Brian Keene

deadite
press

DEADITE PRESS
P.O. BOX 10065
PORTLAND, OR 97296
www.DEADITEPRESS.com

AN ERASERHEAD PRESS COMPANY
www.ERASERHEADPRESS.com

ISBN: 978-1-62105-216-6

Printed in the USA.

Acknowledgements

This time around, thanks to publishers Paul Goblirsch and the staff of Thunderstorm Books, Jeff Burk and the staff of Deadite Press; technical advisors Kevin Foster, Abby Wright, Patrick Freivald, Jack Rosenquist, James Monroe, Kelly and Veronica Smith, Scott Goforth; pre-readers Mark Sylva, Tod Clark, and Stephen McDornell; and friends Bryan Smith, John Urbancik, Geoff Cooper, Mike Oliveri, Mikey Huyck, Mary SanGiovanni, Mike Lombardo, Dave Thomas, Bryan Johnson, Sarah Pinborough, Chris Golden, Jim Moore, Dallas Mayr, Tom Monteleone, F. Paul Wilson, Chet Williamson, Joe R. Lansdale, John Skipp, David Schow, Edward Lee, Cassandra Burnham, and my sons.

DEADITE PRESS BOOKS BY BRIAN KEENE

Urban Gothic
Jack's Magic Beans
Take the Long Way Home
Darkness on the Edge of Town
Tequila's Sunrise
Dead Sea
Entombed
Kill Whitey
Castaways
Ghoul
The Cage
Dark Hollow
Ghost Walk
A Gathering of Crows
Last of the Albatwitches
An Occurrence in Crazy Bear Valley
Earthworm Gods
Earthworm Gods II: Deluge
Earthworm Gods: Selected Scenes from the End of the World
The Rising
City of the Dead
The Rising: Selected Scenes from the End of the World
The Rising: Deliverance
Clickers II (with J. F. Gonzalez)
Clickers III (with J. F. Gonzalez)
Clickers vs. Zombies (with J. F. Gonzalez)
Sixty-Five Stirrup Iron Road (with Edward Lee, Jack Ketchum, Bryan Smith, J.F. Gonzalez, Wrath James White, Ryan Harding, Nate Southard, and Shane McKenzie)

This novel was written while listening to heavy doses of AC/DC, The Adorkables, Autopsy, Black Sabbath, Blue Oyster Cult, Body Count, Broken Hope, Charred Walls of the Damned, Cypress Hill, Dot Com Intelligence, Faith No More, Flatliner, The Gaslight Anthem, Halestorm, Ice-T, Kasey Lansdale, Michael Withers, Orchid, Pentagram, The Police, Shooter Jennings, Sick of It All, Willie Nelson, Witch Mountain, Xander Harris, and YOB (in case you need a soundtrack).

This one is for Cathy and Hannah...

PART ONE

MEET THE NEIGHBORS

One

Sam:
Apartment 1-D

When everyone starts killing each other, Sam doesn't notice at first because he's too busy preparing to kill himself. Samuel L. Miller is pushing fifty and still struggling with the type of financial debt most people have escaped from by the time they reach their mid-thirties. He lives alone because his girlfriend left him and he can't afford another one, and because he never had children with either of his ex-wives, and also because his dog died a week ago.

Sam doesn't miss having a girlfriend. He was never much on talking or sharing, and if he's horny, there's always internet porn. He doesn't miss his ex-wives, except when he's been drinking.

But he misses that dog.

The dog, Sergio, is currently being kept at the Leader's Heights Veterinary Clinic, where he was put to sleep after inoperable cancer in his guts caused him to stop eating and start shitting and pissing blood. The vet gave Sergio two shots—one to calm him and one to put him to sleep. Sam is a writer by trade, and appreciates a good turn of phrase, but he hates that euphemism. Put to sleep. Euthanasia is what it is. Murder, if you want to be less polite about it.

The vet smiled sadly after administering the dose, and then told Sam in her most sympathetic voice that she'd give them some time together. She left the room, and then it was just the two of them, Sam and Sergio, curled up together on the hard linoleum floor, with bright fluorescent lights glaring from above. Sergio's breathing slowed. He licked Sam's hand. His brown eyes closed. Then his breathing stopped.

11

Sam held him, and cried. Eventually, the vet came back in, expressed her sympathies, and asked Sam how he'd be paying for the procedure. When he learned how much it cost for them to kill his dog, Sam explained that he wouldn't be able to pay until his next royalty check arrived. The vet then informed him that he wouldn't be able to take Sergio home until the bill was paid.

Sam considers that as he loads five hollow point rounds into his Taurus .357. If he kills himself now, who will claim Sergio's body? Who will bury him? But then it occurs to Sam that the same questions apply to his own corpse, and he decides that it doesn't matter. He has a sister, Laura, whom he hasn't spoken to in over a year, as well as his brother-in-law, Mike, and their son, Hunter. Sam likes his nephew okay. He's always gotten along well with kids and animals. It's people who he has trouble with. Among Sam's papers are his will and literary estate, assigning the rights to all of his work to Hunter. Unfortunately, any money earned will first have to go toward paying Sam's outstanding debts, the first of which is the Internal Revenue Service, so it's doubtful Sam's post-mortem book royalties will put his nephew through college.

Sam also has two elderly parents who never miss a chance to let him know what a disappointment he has been, be it not providing them with grandchildren, or having two marriages end in flames (his mother is close with both ex-wives and still stays in touch with them), or wasting his time in a career that provides no 401K, no retirement, no health insurance, and is only of interest to them on the extremely rare occasions when Sam or his books are mentioned in *The New York Times* or on *FOX News*, at which point they gloat to their friends about how proud they are of him, their son, the writer.

Fuck it, Sam thinks. *They can bury me and Sergio both. Let them make the arrangements.*

The bullets seem heavier than they normally do. His hands are sweating, and although the bullets feel cool, the oil on his fingers makes them slippery. He manages to slide one into the chamber. The second bullet tumbles from his grasp and lands on the carpet. Sam pauses, debating with himself. Does he really need to load all five chambers? One bullet should suffice. Unless he fucks this up, too, and blows the side of his face off. He's read about such mishaps—people like himself who eat a bullet, but instead of blowing their brains out the back of their head, the bullet travels around their skull and exits out the other side, leaving them a vegetable or a disfigured freak for the rest of their miserable lives.

He decides that he'd better load all five chambers, just in case.

He slides bullets into chambers two, three, and four, and then leans forward on the couch. The brown cushions are covered in dog hair, all that remains of Sergio. He hasn't been able to bring himself to clean them up. The couch is a leftover from his last girlfriend. She left it behind, along with everything else, including him. They met at a book signing. She'd been a fan of his work. Before she moved out, she told Sam that while the fantasy of dating a dark, brooding writer was tantalizing, the reality of being in a relationship with a high-functioning sociopath was anything but.

Sam has never blamed her. He doesn't like living with himself either. And in another few minutes, he won't have to.

Something bangs outside. The noise makes him jump. Sam's grip on the pistol twitches. He's glad he didn't have his finger on the trigger. It wouldn't do to start shooting without first putting the gun in his mouth.

The noise is followed by laughter—a man and a woman. Sam caught a glimpse of them earlier, a young couple in their twenties, fresh out of college by the looks of them (and Sam is usually pretty good at studying people and discerning things about them), with a small kid. They're moving in next door, and they've parked a big rental box truck in the spot where Sam's car used to be, until it was repossessed earlier today for late payments.

Sam puts the handgun on the coffee table. Like the couch, it's a leftover from his previous relationship. A few stray dog hairs cling to this, as well.

A police siren wails. The sound is distant. As it fades, it is answered by another.

He roots around on the stained, thin, coffee-colored carpet, searching for the last bullet. Like everything else in this shithole, the carpet was new back in the early eighties, when the Pine Village Apartment Complex was built. The same goes for the kitchen appliances and the bathroom fixtures. The blinds over the windows are new, but only because Sam bought them himself. Everything else is archaic and either broken or failing. The windows are drafty, the water pressure sucks, the bathroom mirror is cracked, the molding around the front door is loose, and the heating takes forever to warm the place. The chipped paint on the walls is a dingy shade of cream, and is about twelve coats thick. If you look closely at the walls you can see hair and dirt embedded in the previous layers of paint, and poorly patched nail holes left over from previous tenants. Insects and spiders are a constant nuisance. He doesn't know how they get in, but they are always present, no matter how many bug bombs he sets off. The Pine Village management say they can't do anything about it other than call an exterminator, a service for which Sam will have to pay the bill for.

The decrepitude extends to the apartment complex's exterior, as well. There's a playground in desperate need of repair, with rotten wood planks and sharp protruding nails, and a tire swing dangling from rusty chains. The area around the garbage dumpsters is a disaster, with trash and debris scattered across the pavement. Other tenants leave the dumpster doors open, providing a nightly buffet for raccoons, rats, squirrels, feral cats, homeless people, and other scavengers.

No, Sam decides, he will not miss this dump.

Outside, somebody screams. Sound is a constant factor at the Pine Village Apartment Complex. It comes through the walls and the windows and echoes from the parking lot and other apartments and the alleys and streets. When the scream is not repeated, he assumes that nothing is amiss. Screams are a normal sound here at the Complex. So are shrieks, laughter, shouting in various languages, revving car engines, and booming woofers blasting the garbage that passes for hip-hop and country music these days. Sam remembers when hip-hop was Public Enemy and Ice-T, and when country music was Waylon Jennings and Johnny Cash. These days, every hip-hop song sounds exactly the same, and most country music sounds like eighties pop.

The police sirens continue to shriek and fade, shriek and fade. Then a car alarm begins to whoop. Sam considers getting up to check, but then decides against it. After all, his isn't out there anymore, and in a few minutes, a thief breaking into one of his neighbor's cars won't matter. At least not to him.

He scans the living room, looking at his possessions. A plasma television which is only four years old and already shows ghost images in the upper right hand corner. A DVD player that was new back when most people still bought videotapes. The couches and coffee table, left behind by his last girlfriend. A few framed photographs—Sam signing books for some readers, Sam in a bar with some fellow writers, Sam and his first ex-wife, Sam and Sergio at the lake, Sam and Sergio and Sam's second ex-wife. And books. Six cheap pressboard bookshelves bought at Walmart and put together over a long frustrating weekend, crammed with over two-thousand paperbacks, hardcovers, first editions, and signed limited edition collectibles.

In the bedroom, there are six more shelves, also stuffed with books, but these are all ones that have been written by Sam, along with comic books, magazines, anthologies, and other outlets that have featured his work. One shelf contains his literary awards, of which he has many. Last year, Sam was given the Grandmaster Award, one of the highest achievements a writer in his genre could receive. He'd been proud, but twenty-four hours after receiving it, he'd seriously considered selling the award on eBay in order to pay the rent. Awards were nice, but money was nicer. Sadly, a long time ago somebody in his field had apparently decided bronze and plaster busts were better than cash.

The bedroom also has a cheap, pressboard desk (purchased the same weekend Sam bought the shelves). His laptop and printer occupy the desk, along with stacks of miscellaneous papers receipts, and dirty coffee cups. The laptop is on its last leg. It takes forever to start, and the battery only lasts a few minutes when it's not plugged in, and the question mark key doesn't work. Anytime Sam wants to type a question mark into a manuscript he's working on, he has to go online, find an image of a question mark, and then copy and paste it into the document. The bedroom also has a bed, which is nothing more than a cheap mattress and box spring on an even cheaper frame and headboard, haphazardly screwed together and shoved into one corner.

Sam realizes that the only things of value that he owns are the books and the handgun. Everything else is shit. The handgun will probably be taken as evidence after the police investigate his death. But what of the books? Will his relatives claim them? They've never shown any interest in them before, so why would they after his death? He imagines that whatever belongings aren't claimed by his next of kin will be unceremoniously tossed in the dumpsters by the Pine Village Apartment Complex management. He's seen this happen before, almost on a weekly basis. Someone doesn't pay rent, the sheriff puts a notice on their apartment door, and they abscond in the night, leaving behind their belongings, which management then tosses in the dumpsters. He's seen furniture, bedding, toys, and even electronics equipment thrown away in such a manner, and has also seen his neighbors dumpster diving for it all after management has left. He thinks about his books filling up a dumpster, and the illiterate tenants picking through them, looking for DVDs or videogames because nobody reads anymore. For a brief moment, this image is almost enough to make Sam reconsider his decision.

But then, shrugging, he reaches for the gun. No sense delaying the inevitable.

He wonders if it will hurt.

Before he can go any farther, the screams outside start up again.

This time, they don't stop.

Two

Terri and Caleb: Apartment 2-D

"Caleb," Terri calls, "where did you go?"

"I'm right here, Mom."

The six-year old stomps out of the truck, obviously enjoying the sound his feet make on the long metal ramp extending from its rear. Terri wonders what he's pretending to be this time. The Hulk, perhaps? Or maybe a Stormtrooper from *Star Wars*? Mom logic says that it has to be a character who stomps.

Caleb carries a cardboard box. Printed on the side of the box in black magic marker with the particular, painstaking scrawl of a six-year old still learning to write, is 'CALEBS ROOM.' He hauls it through the open apartment door just as Randy comes back outside. Grinning, Randy ruffles Caleb's hair.

"You're pretty strong, little man."

"I know," Caleb says, not bothering to stop, and—Terri notes—also not bothering to look up at Randy. "I got my powers from a gamma-irradiated arc reactor. Now I'm Iron Hulk."

Well, Terri thinks. *Now I know who he's pretending to be.*

A police siren shatters the moment. It is followed by a second one, coming from a different direction, judging by the sound.

"Sounds like a busy evening," Randy quips.

Caleb seems undeterred by the sirens. He reemerges from the apartment and continues to stomp around the parking lot.

The depth of her son's imagination pleases and amazes Terri every single day. He's in first grade, but reading at a

18

third grade level. He does okay in math, as well. Indeed, the only thing Caleb struggles with at school is playing with other kids. He gets frustrated when the other little boys don't want to play whatever it is Caleb wants to play, or don't want to play it the way he wants to, and as a result, he often ends up playing by himself. And although he's okay with the little girls chasing him on the playground, he doesn't like it when they try to hold his hand, and he especially doesn't like it when they tell him they're going to marry him some day. Caleb insists that the only girl he's ever going to marry is his Mommy. Terri sometimes worries about this. While it's normal for little boys to want to marry their mothers, she thinks perhaps he should have outgrown it by this age. She also worries about his tendency to play by himself if the other kids don't want to do what he's doing.

Caleb is an only child—her only child. He has never known his father. In truth, Terri didn't know Caleb's father very well, either. He died before Caleb was born. Terri met the father, Mark, in college. They had five dates, and then she got pregnant. Mark was killed in a drunk driving accident before she ever got a chance to tell him. She reached out to his parents instead, but they wanted nothing to do with her. She has tried contacting them a few times over the years, wanting to offer them an opportunity to know their grandson. They have never responded.

Terri dropped out of college and had Caleb. They've been together ever since. They moved in with her mother, who watched him during the day while Terri worked, and then left for her job as a night nurse when Terri got home. And while that arrangement has mostly been pleasant, and while Terri will always be grateful to her mother for the help, it is time that she and Caleb lived on their own. There are little inconveniences—little battles—like when her mother contradicts Terri's punishment or rules for Caleb. But there is also the fact that her mother is interested in dating a co-worker, a "nice male nurse named Dave", and it's hard for her to do that when her daughter and grandson both live with her. In truth, it's hard for Terri to have any kind of social life either, not that she's really been interested in one. For the last six years, her life has revolved around her son, and she's fine with that. It rarely occurs to her to date, except when her friends try to convince her to sign up for one of the various dating websites or attempt to fix her up with one of their friends. Their Facebook profiles are full of pictures of them and their boyfriends, or, in an increasing number of cases, their husbands. Terri's is full of pictures of Caleb. And a few of her mother. But none of her father. Her father died when she was six-years old. Terri grew up without a father.

Just like her son is doing now.

And that breaks her heart, and she keeps thinking maybe she *should* date again, that maybe she should begin the application process for, let's face it, a father for her son. Deep down inside, she knows that's what it would be. She can't imagine loving someone else the way she loves Caleb. She can't fathom somebody else sharing space in their lives, or a place in her heart. She doesn't need a man in her life, but she worries that her little boy just might. Terri knows all too well how hard it was for her, growing up without a father. She has to assume it's even more difficult for a boy.

Terri frowns, wondering what some of her feminist friends from college would make of her musings. Then she decides that she really doesn't care. Yes, she's doing a fine job of raising Caleb, and no, he doesn't *need* a father figure in his life, but—arguments about gender politics, patriarchy, and sexism aside—it would be nice if he had one anyway.

Randy would fit the bill. They've been friends—best friends—for years, but it's no secret that he wants more from their relationship. She's helped him through two break-ups with two serious girlfriends, and he's helped her by listening and being there for her and Caleb, and one time they even fell asleep together on the couch while watching a movie, but they've never gone beyond that. She loves Randy, the way one loves a dear, dear friend, but her feelings for him are just that—friendship. She's told him many times that there's no chance of a romantic entanglement, no possibility of being friends with 'benefits.' Randy swears that he understands and is okay with it, but sometimes, Terri wonders if that's really true. Sometimes, she feels guilty, feels that maybe she's leading him on. He promises her that she's not, that he's just not into dating anyone right now, and enjoys just hanging out with her and Caleb. But Terri is concerned that, in doing so, he might miss his chance at something more with someone else.

She also wonders sometimes how she'd feel if he got that chance with someone else.

"You okay?" Randy asks, tromping down the ramp with another armload of boxes.

Terri smiles. "Yeah. I'm sorry. I got distracted for a moment."

Shrugging, Randy returns the smile. "No worries. You look beat. We've been at this all day. Why don't you take a break?"

"No." Terri shakes her head. "I want to get this finished. I'm sure you've got better things to do tonight than help me move."

"I can't think of any."

His smile grows broader. He takes the last few steps down the ramp, and stumbles. The top box on the stack he's carrying falls onto the ramp with a loud clang.

"Shit! I'm sorry, Terri."

"It's okay," she assures him. "It's full of Christmas decorations from my Aunt Hildy. I never put them up because they're too gaudy. If you broke them, you'll have done me a favor."

Randy performs a mock bow, and almost drops the rest of the boxes. He catches his balance, and they both laugh. There is a pause, as they look at each other. Terri feels a warmth of emotion in that moment. She suspects that Randy feels something, too. He starts to say something else, but then Caleb emerges from the open apartment door, and walks toward them.

"It's getting dark, Mom."

Terri glances up at the sky, and indeed, it is getting dark. Night is falling, and there is still so much to do. Luckily, they have already unloaded the big furniture. Some of their friends helped with that earlier. But there are still several rows of boxes to haul off the truck, not to mention unpacking, setting up the beds, and returning the truck to the rental agency so she doesn't get charged for another day.

"Let's take five," Randy says. "Caleb, you're in charge of making sure your mom takes a break."

Caleb nods. He still doesn't look Randy in the eye, but he's grinning.

"I'm fine," she insists. "Unless you want to sleep on the floor tonight, Caleb, we've got to get this done. And we still have to return the truck or they'll charge us for another day."

"I'll take care of that," Randy says. "You just make..."

He trails off, staring over her shoulder. Caleb is doing the same. Confused, Terri turns around slowly. At first, she doesn't comprehend what she's seeing. Across the apartment complex's parking lot, there is a small strip of gnarled trees and crooked saplings. Beyond those trees are a vacant lot, and a row of garages with peeling paint and sagging roofs. A shockingly obese man plods across the vacant lot toward them. As she watches, he pushes past the trees. It is then that Terri realizes he is naked. She screams in surprise.

"What the hell?" Randy wobbles on his feet, still holding the boxes.

"It's a tick-tock man," Caleb says.

Terri doesn't understand what her son means. She's too stunned by the fat man's appearance. He's like those people you sometimes read about in news stories, so morbidly obese that when they suffer a medical crisis, it takes rescue workers and a construction crew just to remove them from their house. The difference is that this person is apparently still mobile, and not via a scooter or motorized device. No, he's walking on his own two legs. Those legs are the size of tree trunks, and remind her of swollen, glistening sausage links. Terri suddenly feels queasy.

The fat man strides with purpose—a purpose unknown to her, but clearly evident as he emerges from the trees and steps onto the parking lot, barely squeezing his slick, naked bulk between two parked cars. His massive buttocks smack against one of the vehicles, a red Ford Focus, and the car alarm begins to wail. Lights flash and the horn blares, but the fat man doesn't seem to mind the disturbance.

Caleb does, though. He clasps his hands over his ears and gapes at the naked behemoth. Caleb has always been sensitive to loud, sudden sounds. When he was younger, Terri worried that this might be a sign of autism or Asperger syndrome, but he has been tested for both and pronounced negative. He just doesn't like loud noises. They rarely go to the movies because the volume on the movie trailers cause him discomfort. Caleb prefers to wait for the DVD release, except for the Marvel Cinematic Universe movies, which he'll usually brave in the theatre—because if he doesn't, he'll be left out of the conversation with his friends at school.

"He's a tick-tock man, and...he's naked!" Caleb's voice is thick with a horrible sense of wonder.

The car alarm seems to grow louder. The naked

man continues to plod toward them. Now, at last, Terri understands the strange nickname her son has provided for him. The man's head nods back and forth, side to side, as he walks, and the motion is very much like the pendulum of the grandfather clock in her mother's living room. Now that she's noticed it, Terri has a hard time seeing anything else. The man stares at them with emotionless eyes, head swaying. Tick. Tock. Tick. Tock.

"You guys go inside," Randy says, setting the boxes down. Terri has to struggle to hear him over the alarm. "I don't like the look of this."

Understatement of the year, Terri thinks. There is nothing likeable about the look of this strange intruder. She can hear his labored, heavy breathing even from this distance. His gelatinous body jiggles with each methodical step, and he glistens with sweat. His penis is almost nonexistent, just a tiny nub lost in the folds of flab hanging down from his waist. His smooth, hairless skin is almost fish-belly white, except for a small Hello Kitty tattoo above his left nipple. She almost laughs at the bizarreness of this, but then she notices the machete clutched in his hand. It had been hidden before, concealed in the shadows between the cars. Now, it gleams dully, reflecting the light spilling from one of her neighbor's windows.

"Mommy…"

"Go inside, honey." Terri moves over to Caleb, putting herself between her son and the oncoming obesity.

"Both of you go inside," Randy says. There is an edge to his voice that Terri has never heard before. "And call 911."

"Randy, what are you—?"

Ignoring her, Randy steps forward, approaching the naked man. The stranger doesn't break stride, nor does he show any reaction. He merely continues toward them, closing the distance.

"Randy," Terri calls, and then grabs Caleb's hand tightly.

"Come on, Caleb. Let's get inside. Now!"

Caleb doesn't argue or protest. Indeed, he seems to be the one pulling her as he turns toward the apartment. Terri glances back over her shoulder in time to see Randy confront the fat man.

"Listen, friend, I don't know if you're high on bath salts or something, but—"

He never finishes, because Tick-Tock (as she thinks of him now) raises the machete—stretching his Hello Kitty tattoo—and swings the weapon down in a vicious arc. She hears the sound the blade makes as it cleaves through Randy's skull. When she was a kid, Terri's parents would get bushels of Maryland crabs in the summer. Then they'd spread newspaper out over the picnic table, crack the shells with a wooden hammer, and pry them apart to get at the meat. Randy's skull makes that same sound. Then, the machete's trajectory curves to the side, cleaving through Randy's head and exiting just above his left ear.

His eyes meet Terri's. He opens his mouth to speak and blood pours from his lips.

"Terri...I..."

Randy jitters for a moment, his shirt turning wet with blood, and then part of the top half of his head slides down his shoulder. He stands there, trying to speak, bleeding and dying, missing a quarter of his head, but unable to fall.

Terri screams.

Caleb shrieks.

Tick-Tock pushes Randy over. Randy slams into the pavement, arms and legs sprawled like noodles. The brains left inside of his cloven skull splatter across the blacktop like some garish Rorschach painting made from oatmeal. Steam rises from the gore.

Finally, the car alarm falls silent.

Terri screams again. Her hands flutter to her face. She

doesn't feel it as her own fingernails claw her cheeks. She spins around, grabs Caleb's hand, and flees for their apartment.

Grinning, his head still ticking from side to side, the naked fat man raises the dripping machete and plods after them.

Three

Stephanie (Stephen) (Rose): Apartment 3-D

Stephanie doesn't hear the police sirens or the car alarm or the screams, because she's in the bathroom, looking at herself in the mirror. The bathroom's exhaust fan comes on automatically with the light; something that annoys Stephanie to no end. She can understand running the fan when she takes a shower, but she shouldn't need to listen to it rattling and wheezing when she's only brushing her teeth or putting on make-up. The fan is making that noise now, the motor sputtering and the blades sounding like they have a small rodent trapped between them, but she barely notices.

Instead, she's thinking—not for the first time—that she can no longer see Stephen's reflection in the mirror.

Stephanie has never thought of her birth gender as a separate person, and she doesn't really do so now, either, but she has noticed that she's prone to studying her facial features with a strange, discomforting sort of nostalgia. She's not having doubts about her decision. Indeed, Stephanie has never been more certain of anything in her life. And even if she was uncertain, it would be too late now. She's been undergoing the medical transitioning for the past three and a half years. She's been open about the process, and has received support and encouragement from most of her family and friends. But still…it's strange to look at your reflection in the mirror and see the person you really are staring back at you, rather than the person who you used to be.

Her face is different now, in structure and shape. Her skin is smoother. Her complexion has changed. When she looks at pictures of who she was, versus who she is now, she can still see elements of her old self, but they are muted.

For twenty-two years, she was Stephen.

Now, she is Stephanie.

Who she'd like to be, however, is Rose.

The transition has been hard work. Stephanie has spent the last three and a half years growing her hair out, and working on her body language and voice. She's even worked with a speech therapist who specializes in transgendered clients. She has taken a hormone regimen and watched in wonder, bemusement, and occasionally fear as the estrogen and anti-androgen have redesigned her body, shrinking muscles, changing the look and feel of her skin, adding new shapes and curves, and redistributing fat. She has been surprised at the more subtle changes the hormones have worked on her emotions, as well, to the point where even certain television commercials can make her cry. She has undergone numerous hours of excruciating electrolysis, and has suffered through painful calcium aches common with the transition. She has marveled over how her breasts have grown, satisfactorily enough that she has decided against breast implants—at least for now. She has considered facial feminization surgery, but has been urged by her doctor to wait, and give the hormones more time to work. And for the most part, they have.

There have been other hurdles, too. She has constantly struggled with the gender-specific social conditioning that exists all around her, permeating society, and has felt at times like she is still caught between two worlds, even though most of the process is now over. She has spent time discovering what style of clothing compliments her, and what doesn't. She has worked hard to stop automatically heading for the men's room when in public, and course-correcting for the women's restroom instead.

She has undergone all this and, for the most part, has received nothing but love, support, patience, and understanding from her family and friends. But there is one thing (besides sexual reassignment surgery) that she cannot bring herself to do.

And that is to call herself Rose.

Rose is who she has always wanted to be. Early in the process, when she first spoke about it with her parents, and informed them of her decision, she'd taken to calling herself Stephanie. She'd thought, at the time, that it might make the entire transition easier on her parents, and it has. But they've been so awesome about everything else, and have taken to it so wholeheartedly, that she's afraid to change her name again. Stephanie, after all, is just a variation of her birth name—a name they gave her. A name they obviously liked. Rose is something entirely different. Stephanie realizes this is illogical, but she can't help it. As she recently explained to a friend of hers, it feels like Stephanie was trapped inside Stephen for all those years, but now Rose is trapped inside Stephanie, like a series of Russian nesting dolls.

Sighing, Stephanie turns away from the mirror, thinking that maybe she'll try talking to her parents about it this weekend. She goes over to their house every Saturday to visit and do laundry, because the laundry facility here at the Pine Village Apartment Complex is filthy and decrepit, like something out of a post-apocalyptic movie. Half of the machines don't work, and the ones that do are caked with grime and hair and detergent residue. The dryers are no better. During her first week living here, she found what appeared to be the flea-ridden remnants of a mouse nest in one of the lint traps. Plus, the washing machines cost $1.50 for a load and the dryers are $1.75 for sixty minutes. It costs more to do the laundry here than it costs her in gas to do it at her parent's house.

She turns off the light and the exhaust fan rumbles to a stop and then falls silent. That's when she hears the car alarm blaring and people screaming. She recognizes the sound of the vehicle alarm. It's hers.

Frowning, she hurries down the hall to the living room. She noticed a moving van parked outside earlier today. She wonders if the new tenants are fighting. That would suck. The previous tenant was a quiet divorced father who she never heard and barely ever saw.

The renter on the other side of that until-recently-vacant apartment is Sam, the writer. Stephanie has talked with him a few times, exchanging pleasantries. Although she has never told Sam this, Stephanie tried reading one of his books, after she saw some friends talking about him on Tumblr. She was disappointed. His stuff is definitely not her cup of tea. The book she sampled took place on an island, and had monsters and some pretty graphic violence and several particularly horrific rape scenes. Extreme violence and rape aren't necessarily triggers for her, but neither are they something she wants to read about or watch. Stephanie prefers comics by Kelly Sue DeConnick and Alex de Campi, books by Neil Gaiman and Chuck Wendig, and television shows like *Sherlock* and *Doctor Who*. She is especially fond of the latter. Stephanie has always found comfort in the Doctor's ability to regenerate into a new body.

Her neighbor on the other side is Mrs. Carlucci. She's a nice enough old lady, although Stephanie strongly suspects that she disapproves of Stephanie's transition. Mrs. Carlucci has never come right out and said this, unlike some other people—strangers and a few casual acquaintances—who have unfortunately done so. But still, the looks Mrs. Carlucci gives her speak silently of disapproval. Despite this, Stephanie likes the old lady, because she sometimes bakes cookies and gives them to her neighbors, and also because she's quiet. The only time Stephanie hears her through the walls is when Mrs. Carlucci is feeding her four cats. The Pine Village management only allows for one cat per apartment, but so far, Mrs. Carlucci has gotten around that lease restriction.

Stephanie grabs her keys off the shelf next to the front door and presses a button on the fob. The car alarm stops. She hears a door slam in the apartment next to hers. She sets the car keys back down on the shelf and is about to open the door and look outside, when the screams start again, louder this time. They're coming from right on the other side of the wall. Definitely the new neighbors. They sound like a woman and a kid. Then, a series of loud thuds reverberate through the building as someone begins pounding on the shrieking neighbor's door. Stephanie decides that it might not be safe to open her door. Instead, she grabs her cell phone from its charger on the end table, pondering whether or not she should call 911, and then moves to the kitchen window. She parts the curtains and blinds with her free hand, and peeks outside, trying very hard not to be seen. Her eyes widen in shock.

There is an obscenely fat, naked man banging on her new neighbor's door with the handle of a bloodstained machete. His head ticks back and forth, reminding her of a bobble head figure. At first, she thinks he has a small birthmark on his chest but then she realizes the splotch is a Hello Kitty tattoo.

She notices that someone is lying in the parking lot behind the fat man. She can only see the person's legs and rump. The rest of the body is concealed behind a car. Whoever it is, they aren't moving.

Both the pounding and the screams get louder. Hands trembling, Stephanie lets the shades fall shut and unlocks her phone. She dials 911 and brings the phone to her ear, realizing as she does so that she is hyperventilating. She struggles to get her breathing under control as the emergency dispatcher answers.

"York County Nine One One. What's your emergency?"

"I...there's..." Stephanie's voice trembles. "There's a naked man with a knife trying to break into my neighbor's apartment. I think he may have...killed someone. Or at least hurt them."

"Can you confirm the address, ma'am?"

Stephanie is so scared that she doesn't even feel the momentary sense of happiness she usually gets whenever somebody calls her 'Ma'am.' She does notice, however, that there seem to be a number of phones ringing in the background, and assumes it must be a busy evening at the call center.

"It's the Pine Village Apartment Complex in Red Lion. Apartment 2-D. And I'm in apartment 3-D. Please, hurry."

"I'm alerting police now, ma'am. There's a lot of activity tonight."

"What do you mean? What kind of activity?"

Instead of answering, the dispatcher asks, "Can you stay on the line with me so I can get some more information?"

"Sure."

"Thank you. Can you..."

The dispatcher pauses. At first, Stephanie thinks the call must have been disconnected, but that can't be right, because she can still hear the phones ringing in the background. Then the woman comes back online.

"I'm sorry about that, Ma'am. We've been getting an unusual amount of calls in the last ten or fifteen minutes, and now, apparently there's a disturbance in our lobby. I was distracted for a moment."

"That's okay," Stephanie says.

Next door, the pounding has ceased. It is followed by the sound of glass breaking. The screams grow frantic now.

"Hurry," she says. "I think he just broke a window."

The dispatcher doesn't answer.

"Are you there? Hello?"

Stephanie hears more glass breaking, but this time, she realizes, it's on the other end of the phone.

The dispatcher shouts, "Hey, what are you—"

Something booms on the other end of the line. Stephanie thinks it might be a gunshot. The dispatcher yells. The boom is followed by three more. Then the call ends.

"Oh my God…"

She stares at the phone, blinking. When she tries calling back, she gets a message telling her that her call cannot be completed as dialed.

"How can it not be completed as dialed? I'm calling 911!"

She listens for the sound of approaching police sirens, but all she hears are more screams from next door, now at a fevered pitch. After a moment's debate, Stephanie puts the phone down on the counter and grabs a butcher knife instead. Terrified, she opens the front door, just enough to stick her head outside. Then she gasps. Her eyes widen.

More naked people are trudging out of the woods and into the parking lot. Some of them are carrying knives. One of them has a bloodstained axe. Another is armed with a weed whacker. A few carry nothing but are equipped with crazed, slavering grins. And then the fat man, who is apparently too large to squeeze through the broken window next door, turns toward her. Shards of broken glass crunch under his bare feet. He doesn't seem to notice.

Stephanie is frozen in place. She forgets about the butcher knife in her hand. She doesn't think to close the door and lock it. She simply stares, paralyzed with fear, watching his head twitch back and forth, back and forth, as he raises the machete and trudges toward her, leaving bloody footprints on the sidewalk.

Four

Mrs. Carlucci:
Apartment 4-D

Mrs. Edna Carlucci has no patience for nonsense. Fighting neighbors, screaming children, loud music, or teenagers squealing their tires in the parking lot—these things constitute nonsense, and nonsense is not to be tolerated. Mrs. Carlucci believes you should be respectful of your neighbors at all times. Don't get involved with their business. Don't be a snoop or a gossip. Be friendly. Say hello. Stay on good terms. Don't be disruptive or a nuisance. Don't drive like a maniac through the parking lot. Carry your trash to the dumpsters between buildings A and B, rather than letting it sit outside your door. Clean up your dog poop. Keep the volume on your television and radio at a responsible level. Do unto others as you would have them do unto you. Don't engage in nonsense.

So, when she hears the screams and the car alarm, her first reaction isn't panic or fear. Instead, she is angry. While some of the other buildings in the complex have rowdy tenants, the D-building has always been relatively quiet and peaceful. She doesn't really know any of her neighbors that well—not like the old days, when she was a young girl, and everybody on the street knew everybody else. Those days are gone. These days, a person is lucky if they get a nod of acknowledgement when passing by a neighbor outside. Neighbors aren't really neighbors anymore. They're strangers, for the most part.

She knows the young girl next door. Stephanie is her name. Mrs. Carlucci isn't sure, but she thinks Stephanie might be one of those Trans people she's seen on the TV.

And if so, that's okay. As long as she's not hurting anybody else, she can be whatever she wants to be. Still, Mrs. Carlucci sometimes gets nervous around Stephanie, because she's unsure how to refer to Stephanie, or whether or not she should inquire about the process. She would like to. She would very much like to understand it more. But she's not sure if asking Stephanie about it would be polite.

She also knows the man three apartments down. His name is Sam. Mrs. Carlucci isn't sure what he does for a living, but he never seems to go to work. Maybe he works from home, or perhaps he has an inheritance—although, if he's living here at the Pine Village complex, it must not be much of one. Sam always inquires about her cats, which is nice. He recently had his dog put to sleep, and was quite upset. Poor man. Mrs. Carlucci made sure to buy him a sympathy card. She knows how devastated she would feel if something happened to one of her four cats—Princess, Queenie, King, and Hannibal. King came to her as a stray, a black-and-white Maine Coon kitten who showed up beneath her car one summer morning. Princess and Queenie are shelter adoptees, she took in as kittens. Hannibal is also a shelter adoptee, although he came to her as an adult. His previous owners—a young couple and their daughter—all died in a house fire. Mrs. Carlucci has done her best to make him feel at home, and he seems to tolerate both her and the other cats, but sometimes, late at night, he sits on the sill of the living room window and stares out into the dark, and she is certain he misses his other owners.

Mrs. Carlucci worries a lot about her cats. She fears what will happen to them when she is gone, and at her age, that's more of an inevitability than a possibility. Her doctor says she is in good health, and jokes that she will outlive him, but her doctor is prone to nonsense, and Mrs. Carlucci doesn't like him very much. She preferred her old physician, Dr.

Hammond, but he passed away five years ago. Most of her friends have also passed. These days, it's just her and her cats. One day soon, it will just be the cats. What will become of them? Will one of the neighbors take them in?

In the apartments below her, accessible from the other side of the building, there is a nice young married couple that always smile and nod, but she doesn't know their names. And, of course, there's Mr. Hicks, a widower or a bachelor. She can't be sure which. He is friendly with her, but she knows what he has in mind, and she is not interested. And it's not because he's black, or ugly. Indeed, he's quite handsome for a man his age. But Grady Hicks could be Robert Redford or Sidney Poitier and she still wouldn't be interested. She hasn't been interested in anyone since Mr. Carlucci, God rest his soul, went to be with the Lord ten years ago next May.

Mrs. Carlucci begins and ends every day down on her knees at the foot of the bed, hands clasped in fervent prayer to God and the Holy Mother, hoping that she will be reunited with Mr. Carlucci soon.

And that when she is, someone will watch over her cats.

She doesn't know which neighbor is making all this noise, but it sounds like somebody is being murdered. King, who has been perched at the kitchen window, leaps down and darts for the bedroom, his fur standing straight up. Queenie and Princess follow his lead, perhaps sensing his alarm. Hannibal remains sprawled out on the sofa in the living room, but his ears are up and his eyes are alert.

Frowning, Mrs. Carlucci goes to the kitchen window and peeks outside. Her eyes widen in stunned disbelief. There are naked people running across the parking lot towards Stephanie's apartment. *Naked people!* This is the biggest instance of nonsense Mrs. Carlucci has ever experienced, in all her years living at Pine Village. They seem quite agitated about something. Then she realizes that not only are they nude, but many of them seem to be carrying weapons. As she watches, one of them pauses in the middle of the parking lot and pulls the starter cord on a gas-powered weed whacker. The engine chortles, then sputters. Lips curled back in a snarl, the naked man tries again. This time, the weed whacker roars to life, belching tiny puffs of blue-gray smoke from its exhaust. Its wielder joins the throng of other naked people, all of whom seem to be heading for Stephanie's front door.

Reeling, Mrs. Carlucci backs away from the window. Her hands are tingling and her lips feel numb. There is a heaviness in her chest, and she wonders if she is having a heart attack. Her first thought is to turn to the four food dishes and large water bowl on the floor next to the refrigerator, and make sure that there is enough food and water for the cats. Who knows how long it will take someone to find her? She doesn't want Princess, Queenie, King, and Hannibal to starve in the meantime.

She hears Stephanie scream next door, but the sound is curiously muted. So, too, are the noises the crowd is making outside. After a moment, Mrs. Carlucci realizes this is because her ears are ringing. Her skin feels flush, and the tingling in her hands increases, running up her arms and into her shoulders. Her hand flutters to her chest. She feels her pulse, thrumming beneath her skin. Has it ever felt so strong or so rapid? Mrs. Carlucci doesn't think so.

Something soft brushes against her leg, just below the hem of her dress, and Mrs. Carlucci squawks with fright. She reaches for the wall to keep from falling. Glancing down, she sees Hannibal. The cat looks alert and angry. His muscles are taut beneath his fur. He glances up at her, and the ringing in her ears subsides.

"Hannibal," she gasps, "you fool cat! You nearly tripped me."

Mrs. Carlucci leans against the wall, catching her breath.

Slowly, the tingling in her arms and face begins to subside. Not a heart attack, she decides. More likely just panic. With caution, she reaches down and scratches the cat on top of his head, right between his ears. This usually elicits a deep purr from Hannibal, but now, he barely seems to notice. His attention is focused on the wall—on the other side of which is Stephanie's apartment.

Moving slowly, because her legs feel weak and she doesn't trust them, Mrs. Carlucci shuffles toward the phone mounted on the wall between the kitchen and the living room. She doesn't own a cell phone, and has never even used one. She's familiar with them from television, and seeing other people with them. Indeed, it seems like everybody these days owns a cell phone. She sees people with them at the grocery store every week, and at the park where she stops once a week to feed the ducks, and everywhere else. Most heartbreaking—or perhaps annoying—are the parents with cell phones, their attention focused on the tiny screens instead of their own children. More nonsense.

Mrs. Carlucci fumbles with the receiver and manages to lift it from the cradle. She brings the phone to her ear and hears a dial tone. Silently thanking God and the Holy Mother, she dials 911. There is a pause, and then she gets a recorded message informing her that the call cannot be completed as dialed. She feels her panic start to return, and glances down at Hannibal in an effort to stay focused. It works, and she feels a sense of resolve. She tries calling again, but now there is no dial tone at all. Instead, she hears a blaring fast busy signal. Apparently, the lines are down. Either that, or they are overloaded. Mrs. Carlucci considers this. If there are naked people with weapons running around all over Red Lion, then it stands to reason that the phone lines are overloaded. Still, the experience is disconcerting, and only adds to her fright. She has only experienced an outage once since living in Pine

Village—during a very long week in January 2014, when the Polar Vortex turned all of Central Pennsylvania into a disaster area, and eight feet of snow and ice, downed trees, and below zero temperatures led to a temporary loss of not just phone service, but electricity and other utilities, as well.

She hangs up the phone as the naked people begin battering Stephanie's door. Glass shatters, and she assumes its either Stephanie's living room or kitchen window. Her breath catches in her throat as she wonders if they'll come to her window next. It occurs to her that Stephanie is no longer screaming. Indeed, she's not making any noise at all. The only sounds now are those of the crowd outside, and the weed whacker. The naked people don't speak. They simply growl and shout.

Mrs. Carlucci hurries out of the kitchen, moving as quietly as she can. Hannibal follows her, but he doesn't entwine himself between her feet. She retreats to her bedroom. Usually, the bedroom smells of cranberry and rose petal potpourri. Now, however, the only thing she can smell is the bitter, ammoniac stench of the two litter boxes in the spare bedroom. With some effort, she kneels on the floor, ignoring the sudden pain that flares up in her knees and lower back, and peers beneath her bed. Queenie, Princess, and King are hiding beneath it, pressed back against the wall. Only their eyes and a tuft of Princess's white fur are visible in the darkness.

"You three stay under there," she tells them.

Hannibal nuzzles her cheek with his nose and meows. Mrs. Carlucci turns to him, purses her lips, and makes a kissing noise. Hannibal responds by pressing his nose against her mouth and purring.

"You stay here, too. Protect the others."

She swears, not for the first time, that Hannibal understands what she's saying. He doesn't crawl underneath the bed to hide with the others, but he does leap up onto the mattress and position himself on the comforter. His eyes remain alert. One corner of his mouth is curled up in a sneer, revealing a long, pointed incisor. His tail whips back and forth in agitation.

"Good boy."

He meows once, confirming that he is indeed a good boy, and that it's about time she recognized it.

Groaning, Mrs. Carlucci stumbles to her feet and opens the drawer on her nightstand. Inside is Mr. Carlucci's Colt .45 revolver. He taught her to fire it many years ago, and she used to accompany him to the range twice a year to practice shooting at cans. She has not held it since he passed. She pulls the weapon from the drawer. It feels cold against her skin, and heavier than she remembered. Mrs. Carlucci keeps the gun loaded, much to the consternation of some of the ladies at her church. But as her husband had always said, what good was an unloaded pistol? If a burglar broke into her apartment, would she ask them to wait while she fumbled with the bullets?

She releases the cylinder, making sure that all six chambers are filled. Then she snaps it back into place. Clutching the pistol in one hand, she reaches down to give Hannibal one last scratch. She runs her index finger beneath his chin. He raises his head and closes his eyes, signaling his contentment, but when she stops, he is immediately alert again.

As Mrs. Carlucci walks out of the bedroom, the fire siren begins to wail. The fire house is six blocks away from the complex, but the siren is loud enough that it regularly wakes her from her sleep. It continues shrieking as Mrs. Carlucci crosses the living room and reaches for the doorknob. She is still terribly frightened, but she is also very calm. The naked people have knives, axes, and a weed whacker, but she has a

40

gun, and she is tired of their nonsense.

She doesn't stop to consider a plan. Her intent is vague. She thinks that perhaps she will scare them off, or manage to somehow hold them at gunpoint until the police arrive. Yes, her land line is out, but surely one of the other tenants has used their cell phones to call the police. She doesn't see herself killing anyone, but she will if she has to. There's no question about it. Stephanie is a nice young woman—or is it young man? And she's a neighbor. Mrs. Carlucci will not allow her to become the victim of some crazed naked mob, probably high on drugs.

Mrs. Carlucci has seen that on the news before—stories about homicidal naked people, under the influence of new designer drugs, breaking into homes and attacking cars on freeways, and in one case, trying to abduct a little girl from a park. She is fairly certain that something similar is happening now. It's the only reasonable explanation. The closest mental health facility is in York, and if the throng outside were escaped from there, it was inconceivable they would have reached Red Lion unstopped. So yes, drugs are probably the culprit. She just hopes they aren't so high that they ignore the fact that she has a gun.

As the fire siren and the weed whacker battle for noise supremacy, Mrs. Carlucci grips the revolver tighter. Then, murmuring a quick prayer, she opens the door and steps outside.

Five

Shaggy and Turo: Apartment 5-D

Shaggy is sprawled out on a stained couch that was rescued from the curb in front of a fraternity house, and Turo is slouched down in a sagging recliner purchased at a yard sale for ten bucks, when they hear the noises erupting from the apartments around the front side of the building. They hear the siren at the fire house. They hear shouts and screams. They hear thuds and bangs. They even hear a sputtering weed whacker. But they don't pay attention to any of these things for several reasons.

First of all, their gaze is focused on the flat screen television that occupies one wall of the living room. It squats atop a black pre-manufactured television stand that is too small to properly hold it. Shaggy and Turo are staring at the screen in dismay, because their Xbox just lost its connection to the internet in the middle of their game.

Also, it's not the first time they've heard any of these sounds around the Pine Village Apartment Complex. Shouting, and sometimes even screaming, occurs regularly. So do thuds and bangs and other noises. And the weed whacker? Well, there's a lawn and garden service that tends to the property once a week (although it doesn't occur to either of them that it's a little too late in the day for someone to be trimming the grass).

But the main reason they haven't really acknowledged the noises coming from the apartments above them, is because both Shaggy and Turo are stoned as fuck.

However, when the gunshots start a few seconds later, that gets their attention.

Shaggy bolts upright on the couch, dropping his video game controller.

"Whitey," he shouts, looking at Turo in alarm.

Panicked, Turo crouches further down into the recliner, as if trying to hide himself in its cushions, and shakes his head.

"Tony and Vince," Turo says. "It's gotta be."

"Shit," Shaggy responds. "What if it's all three of them? What if they're teaming the fuck up?"

They stare at each other for a few seconds, their bloodshot eyes bright with panic. A spent bowl sits in an ashtray on the coffee table, along with a lighter, a plastic bag with six more buds inside of it, twelve empty beer bottles, a crumpled potato chip bag, a half-eaten package of cookies, and several mugs of days-old coffee—the surfaces of which have begun to sprout a thin, scummy layer of mold. Amidst all of this is a Kimber .45 handgun. A full spare magazine lies next to it, loaded with hollow points.

Shaggy slips off the couch, and grabs the weapon with one trembling hand.

"Where's your gun?" he whispers.

Shrugging, Turo shakes his head again. "I don't know. Around here somewhere."

"Well, you better get it, motherfucker. You hear that shit?"

As if to punctuate his query, several more gunshots echo outside. Judging by the sound, there are two weapons, and two different calibers.

Nodding, Turo starts to stand up, but Shaggy gestures wildly at him.

"Duck, you dumb fuck. Don't let them see you at the window. You fixing to catch a bullet?"

"They're on the other side of the building," Turo says. "Up over the hill. And I don't think that creepy Russian fuck

43

would team up with the Italians anyway."

"We stole from them both. I don't see why they wouldn't. Whitey does business with Tony and Vince. Ain't no reason he wouldn't join them in killing some motherfuckers."

"But if it's them, then why are they on the other side of the building? And who the fuck are they shooting at?"

Shaggy pauses, considering this. "Maybe they got the wrong apartment. Or maybe they're asking around about us, and nobody would tell them nothing, so now they're getting fucking rough."

"Or maybe it's not them at all."

"Then who the fuck would it be?"

Turo shrugs. "I don't know. All I know is I'm tired of hiding up in here. What good is that money if we can't go outside to spend it?"

"Shit. We can't spend it till we fucking get it again."

Four days ago, Shaggy and Turo became rich. Unfortunately, they haven't been able to enjoy their newfound wealth.

It all started two months prior when Shaggy got pulled over by the cops—not for speeding or running a red light or ignoring a stop sign or failure to properly signal. Indeed, he'd been doing thirty-five in a forty-five mile per hour zone when he and Turo spotted the swirling blue and red lights behind them. No, Shaggy had been pulled over because the State Trooper's vehicle was equipped with ALPR— Advance License Plate Recognition—a computerized system that automatically scanned the license plates of every car that drove by the cruiser, and alerted the officer inside of any infractions. In Shaggy's case, his crime had been driving without automobile insurance—an automatic infraction in Pennsylvania. It wasn't that he didn't want to have car insurance. It was that he hadn't been able to afford the premiums, and had missed two monthly payments as a result. The insurance company had cancelled his policy, and informed the Pennsylvania Department of Motor Vehicles, and the next thing he knew, there he and Turo stood along the edge of the road. Fifteen minutes earlier, they'd been on their way to work. Instead, they watched as the State Trooper seized Shaggy's license plate at the scene, wrote him a citation, warned them not to drive the car without a plate, and then drove away.

They'd spent their last sixty bucks getting the car towed back to the Pine Village Apartment Complex, and Shaggy had fretted over how to pay the two-hundred and fifty dollar fine, and then he'd gotten a notice in the mail saying his driver's license was suspended for ninety days. And since Turo's license was also suspended for driving while intoxicated six months before, they were fucked.

One night, while stoned, they'd been commiserating about how all of their problems in life stemmed from being broke—a problem that had only been exacerbated by the fact that they'd now lost their jobs because they had no way of getting to work. They'd discussed robbing a bank, a grocery store, and the check cashing place over on Walnut Street. Then they'd considered stealing from Sam, the neighbor who lived above them. The dude wrote horror novels, supposedly, so it was possible he had Stephen King money. They soon decided against this, however, reasoning that if Sam had any money at all, he wouldn't be living in Pine Village.

Then, their friend Ron had offered a plan. An uneasy truce existed between the local Russian and Italian organized crime outfits, who were both struggling against the black gangs and Mexican cartels moving in from Baltimore and Philly. He told them about a strip club called The Odessa, which was owned and operated by an albino Russian gangster named Whitey. According to Ron, two soldiers from the Marano Family—a pair of made men named Tony Genova and Vince Napoli—dropped a bag full of money off there every month. How much money? Ron didn't know for sure, but several friends had told him it was usually upwards of a quarter-million dollars. The next such financial exchange was scheduled for the following week. Stealing it inside the club would be impossible. They'd never make it out alive. But hitting the two mobsters in the strip club's parking lot might be doable.

Shaggy, Turo, and Ron staked out The Odessa, making note of the car the mobsters arrived in, where they parked, and what they did upon exiting the vehicle. In addition to Tony and Vince, there were two other associates. All four were armed, but none of them were carrying openly. The bag full of money was, in fact, a briefcase, and the way Genova clutched it, the contents were certainly valuable.

When their surveillance was finished, the three conspirators had retreated back to Shaggy and Turo's apartment, and hatched their plan. Given that there were four mobsters and only three of them—of which Ron would remain behind the wheel of their car—they needed a fourth person. Ron suggested his brother Jimmy, just out of a six-month stint in county prison and looking for work.

Shaggy and Turo struggled to make the rent for the next month, hustling and stealing and doing whatever they could to hold off the bill collectors and the utility shut-off notices. They talked about what they would do with the money, and tried to hold out. Tried to stay positive and upbeat. It seemed to them that the next exchange would never come, but it did, and everything started out great.

Arriving a few hours early, Ron parked his car four spaces away from where the mobsters had parked the previous month. The four of them went inside the club for a while, so as to not arouse suspicion. The parking lot had security cameras, and it might have seemed odd for the four of them

46

to sit inside the car the entire time. As the expected arrival time drew nearer, the four of them finished their drinks and decided to return to the car.

Unfortunately, they almost missed their window of opportunity. As they exited the club, they nearly ran into Genova, Napoli, and their two associates. The mobsters had arrived early.

"Excuse me," Genova had said, smiling. "My fault."

Then he'd backed up, allowing them to exit through the door.

"Sorry about that," Ron had muttered.

"No worries," Genova insisted. "It was my fault. Should have been watching where I was going."

Shaggy and Turo had glanced at each other, unsure of what to do.

Then, Ron decided for them by punching Genova in his still-smiling mouth. The stunned criminal stumbled backward, arms flailing. Jimmy darted forward and grabbed the briefcase, wrestling it away from the injured man. Then, before the other three mobsters could even draw their weapons, Jimmy took off across the parking lot.

"Come on," Ron shouted, as Shaggy and Turo stood there blinking. "Move your ass!"

Shaggy and Turo raced after Ron and Jimmy. Shouts echoed behind them, but they were too afraid to turn around and see what was happening. They were halfway to the car when Jimmy lurched forward, as if he'd been kicked in the back. Bloody holes appeared in his shirt. A second later, they heard the shots. The briefcase slipped from Jimmy's grasp as he tottered back and forth, weaving unsteadily on his feet. Then the back of Jimmy's head exploded.

Turo slid to a halt and screamed. Shaggy clutched his arm and urged him on. Without stopping, Ron bent over, snatched up the briefcase, and ran for the car. Bullets pinged off the pavement and the surrounding automobiles. Then Shaggy and Turo started running again.

"You boys know who you're fucking with?" Genova shouted.

Ron's car roared to life. Seconds later, the tires squealed as he barreled out of the parking lot, baring down directly on the gangsters. The gunmen scattered as he rocketed toward them, recovering fast enough to shoot out his rear windshield. He screeched out onto the road, his rear bumper banging off the asphalt, and then zoomed away.

By then, Shaggy and Turo had fled through the parking lot of an adjoining Taco Bell, behind a dry cleaners, and into a stretch of woods bordering an industrial park. They ran all night, hiding in culverts and garbage dumpsters, plowing through forests, and racing across highways, fields, and vacant lots. They babbled to one another in shock and fear about Jimmy's fate, and the fact that Ron had abandoned them, and how they were going to get home, and what the hell they would do now.

They'd made it back to Red Lion just before dawn, exhausted, sweaty, and dismayed. Seeing nothing suspicious around their apartment, the two had gone inside. Then Ron called, informing them that he'd stashed the money inside an old iron ore mine out in the woods near LeHorn's Hollow. He apologized for leaving them behind, saying he'd been in shock after seeing his brother gunned down, and wasn't thinking clearly. He assured them he was all better now, and that all they had to do was lay low for a while, and when the coast had cleared, they'd split the money between themselves.

That had been four days ago. Shaggy and Turo have spent much of that time stoned or drunk or both. They've waited to hear from Ron, or the cops, or the people they robbed. So far, they haven't. They've been afraid to go outside, afraid to make a phone call, afraid to do anything but sit and drink and smoke and play video games.

Now, all of that has changed.

"Let's make a break for it," Shaggy says, crouched behind the sofa.

"And go where?" Turo parts the vinyl blinds with one finger and peers out the window. So far, the yard outside their apartment, which borders a small stretch of woodland, is empty.

"I don't fucking know. Anywhere but here!"

"How? We ain't got no fucking car, no fucking driver's licenses, and no fucking money. How far we gonna get?"

Turo lets the blinds fall shut, sinks back down to the floor again, and tries not to cry.

Shaggy stands up, still clutching the .45, and snatches the spare magazine off the table. Then he heads for the door.

"Stay here if you want," he says, "but I'm leaving while I still can. I'm betting they killed Ron, and I'm also betting he fucking gave us up before they did. Probably tortured him and shit."

"Dude, for all we know, Ron took off with the fucking money."

"Bullshit, motherfucker." Shaggy shakes his head. "He wouldn't do that."

"Shaggy, please. Don't go out there."

"I'm fucking going. The question is, are you coming, too, or you gonna stay here and wait to get shot?"

He opens the door. Instead of responding, Turo lurches to his feet and hurries after him. The two creep out of the apartment and glance around. Shaggy eases the door shut behind him, and doesn't bother to lock it. The yard is still empty, but three figures emerge from the nearby woods. All of them are nude. One of them is covered in blood. Another carries a hunting rifle. Spying Shaggy and Turo, the naked gunman raises the stock to his shoulder and aims at them.

"Go!" Shaggy pushes Turo, who is still trying to come to terms with their nudity.

They run around the side of the apartment building as the shot echoes behind them. Too late, they realize they are now running directly toward the sounds of the original chaos. They round the corner and skid to a stop. The parking lot is filled with more naked people, many of whom are armed with a variety of weapons—everything from guns and knives to a frying pan and a weed whacker. There are several dead bodies lying on the pavement. All but one of them is nude. Another naked person is slumped over the hood of a car, bleeding out onto the metal from a gunshot wound to his face. More dead nudists are sprawled in a pile in front of apartment 2-D. That apartment's front windows are busted out and shards of broken glass sparkle on the ground.

Shaggy and Turo's neighbors are also armed. Sam the writer and the old lady that lives three doors down from him both have handguns. As the two would-be stick-up men watch in disbelief, the old lady shoots a naked person in the stomach. The naked person staggers and his mouth curls into a grimace as blood spurts from the wound, but he doesn't drop the axe he's holding until the old lady shoots him a second time.

The tranny who lives in the apartment between Sam and the old lady is standing outside, watching all this go down. She has a butcher knife in one hand, and judging by the blood on the blade, she's recently used it. Shaggy still occasionally gives Turo shit, because Turo once remarked while high that he thought the tranny was "kind of pretty, but not in a gay way." Next to her are a young red-headed woman and a kid, both of whom look like they're in shock. The kid has his hands pressed tight over his ears. His eyes are wide as half dollars. His mother has bitten through her lip, and blood dribbles down her chin, but she seems oblivious to it.

More naked people are converging on the apartment complex, wandering out of the surrounding woods and alleys and backstreets. The other neighbors don't seem to notice, because they're too preoccupied with the closer opponents. They also don't seem to notice as a naked little girl, probably eight or nine years old, charges toward Sam. She's grinning and snarling, and clutches a butcher knife in her hand.

"Look out," Turo yells.

Shaggy is yelling, too—nonsensical words, the language of panic. He raises the .45 and shoots the little girl in the leg. The hollow point round shreds flesh and shatters bone. She spins and falls, crying out in both pain and rage. Her grin is gone, replaced with an indignant expression, as if she can't believe Shaggy just shot her. Shaggy can't believe it himself. His legs are shaking and his mouth has gone dry. When the little girl starts crawling toward Sam, dragging her injured, half-severed leg behind her, his stomach roils at the trail of blood in her wake.

"Inside my apartment," Sam shouts. "All of you…run, goddamn it! Run!"

The redhead and her kid glance around in confusion, and the tranny guides them toward Sam's open door. Sam and the old lady follow, keeping their guns trained on the advancing horde. Shaggy and Turo hurry along after them. The little girl is almost upon Sam now, and Shaggy points at her, unable to speak. Sam scurries out of her way and follows the rest of them into his apartment.

"Move those bookshelves over to the windows," Sam orders, as he slams and locks the door. "Don't worry about the books. Just dump them on the floor. We need to move fast."

"What about the kitchen?" the old lady asks. "You've got windows in there, too."

"We'll use the fridge." As Sam starts toward the kitchen, he glances at Shaggy and Turo. "Don't just stand there. Move!"

"Mommy," the kid wails. "Make them stop!"

Her only response is to sob.

Outside, a chainsaw sputters, chokes, and then roars to life. The naked people begin battering the door. The blows are almost as loud as the gunshots were. The door rattles in its frame, and the knob jiggles, but the lock holds. The rumbling of the chainsaw draws closer.

Turo and Shaggy's eyes meet, as the pounding on the door increases.

"Dude," Turo gasps, breathless. "What the fuck is going on?"

"I don't fucking know," Shaggy replies, "but whatever it is, we're deep in it now."

Six

Grady Hicks:
Apartment 6-D

Grady Hicks hasn't had a dream about Vietnam since 1988. Years of therapy and counseling—not to mention two divorces and three decades of sobriety—have seen to that. And he's not dreaming about his time in Vietnam now, either.

Instead, he's dreaming about what happened to him after he got home.

Grady made it back to the world in April of 1967, but still had a year left on his enlistment. That July, Grady was asleep in his apartment off-base, his first wife resting next to him, when he got a call telling him to muster at his barracks with full gear in an hour. The next thing he knew, Grady and the rest of the 82nd Airborne's 3rd Brigade were on their way to Selfridge Air Force Base near Detroit. Two days later, Governor George Romney and President Lyndon B. Johnson deployed them to help quell the 12th Street race riots.

Grady saw a lot of things during his time in Vietnam— the type of things a person spent the rest of their lives trying to forget. But in some ways, what he saw during those two days in Detroit were worse than the most savage atrocity committed by the Viet Cong. Detroit, and particularly 12th Street, was a war zone. There were storefronts and row-homes instead of bamboo and mud huts, Molotov cocktails rather than punji sticks, concrete instead of rice paddies, and Saturday Night Specials instead of M-16s, but it was a war all the same.

They mustered at a local high school, where Grady and the other black soldiers were given the option of not going out onto the streets. Instead, they were informed that

if they wanted to, they could pull service duty instead—
laundry, kitchen, communications, and other jobs around
the temporary base. Grady had declined, knowing that if he
opted for a support role, he'd never see himself the same
again from the eyes of his fellow soldiers. Maybe they
wouldn't think less of him, but he would expect them to, and
that was just as bad.

And so, armed with rubber bullets and sheaths over their
bayonets, they'd marched out into the city, showing force
and guarding utility workers and emergency responders.
Within two days of their deployment, the riots ended, leaving
more than forty people dead. During those two days, Grady
witnessed police officers—the same police officers he was
there to support—abusing citizens in their custody. He was
attacked by both blacks and whites, and called an Uncle Tom
and a race traitor more times than he could count. Worst of
all was the mindset of the rioters and looters, the frenzied
madness which seemed to claim them all. Their grievances
were legitimate. Grady agreed with them, intellectually and
emotionally. He even empathized—to a point—with their
desire for violence. But what he saw occurring had nothing to
do with justice or revolution or even simple payback. It was
more a pack mentality, an animalistic mindset of violence
for violence's sake—a whirlwind that sucked in everyone it
came into contact with.

That's where he is now. In the dream, Grady is back on
12th Street, being spit upon and taunted by his own people,
being called a sellout, while rape and murder and arson and
looting occur all around him. He smells gasoline and smoke,
hears people screaming, flames crackling, sirens wailing,
and gunshots ringing out in the night, and somewhere behind
it all, a chainsaw roars.

The sounds continue when he wakes, lurching upright in
bed and immediately gritting his teeth at the pain the sudden

movement has spurred in his bad back. Pain flares in his hands and knees, as well—his arthritis letting him know that it's awake, too, and ready for another day.

Wincing, Grady slowly inches to the side of the bed and puts his feet on the floor. He feels disoriented. He takes a nap most evenings, but he doesn't usually wake feeling like this, and he rarely has bad dreams during those naps, either. Outside, the sirens and the drone of the chainsaw continues. Someone screams. Staccato gunshots echo. Grady shakes his head and rubs his eyes. At first, he thinks the sounds of chaos are just leftover impressions from his nightmare, but they don't fade as he comes fully awake. If anything, they get louder.

One of Grady's friends from the war, another black man named Johnny Walker, used to suffer from occasional flashbacks—or at least, he did until ten years ago, when cancer ate him down to nothing. The doctors at the Veteran's Administration said the cancer was from smoking, but Grady knew the truth. Johnny had brought that cancer back home with him from Vietnam, and it had lurked inside of him all that time. Grady has never had a flashback to the war, or to anything else from his time in the army. But he's convinced he's having one now—a flashback of the riots.

His knees pop as he clambers from bed, and his sciatic nerve is as taut as a guitar string, but he ignores the pain, focusing instead on what he's hearing. It all certainly sounds real enough. The sirens have stopped, but the other sounds have definitely increased. His first urge is to call 911, but the phone is all the way in the kitchen. Grady used to have one of those little cellular flip phones, but his arthritis made operating the tiny buttons an exercise in futility, so now he relies on his old-fashioned rotary phone. His daughter, on her twice-annual visits, thinks this is funny. He likes to remind her that arthritis is hereditary. She doesn't find that as amusing as his phone.

Instead of making the call, Grady decides to check the bedroom window. The thought occurs to him that this might still be part of the dream. Grady recently turned seventy, and the shadow of dementia weighs on him. His mother died of Alzheimer's, and in his opinion, burning to death in a burst of clinging napalm would be preferable to that. These days, he's inclined to worry any time he momentarily forgets something, be it putting his keys in the ashtray next to the door where he also keeps his spare change, or the name of the girl he had a crush on in fifth grade. If the sounds aren't real—and how could they be—then...

He takes a deep breath. The gunshots have ceased, but the chainsaw is still buzzing as its operator revs the throttle again and again. The screams have turned to shouts now, and there's a thumping sound overhead, as if someone is moving furniture. It doesn't seem like the commotion is coming from directly overhead, but rather, from apartment 1-D. That's where the writer lives. Grady doesn't know what he writes. Books, he supposes. Or maybe articles. Grady has nodded at the guy in passing, but they've never spoken. He only knows the man is a writer because that's what Tina, Grady's former neighbor, told him. Grady misses Tina. He vastly preferred living next door to her, rather than the two druggies who currently occupy apartment 5-D. Grady isn't exactly sure what kind of drugs they're on. He's smelled pot smoke coming from their apartment before, and he doesn't give a shit about that. Lord knows he's smoked his share over the years. But those two guys are obviously on some heavier stuff. Meth, maybe. Or crack. Or one of those new synthetic drugs he's heard about on the news, which makes people's skin break out in bleeding, open sores, or causes them to overheat, rip off their clothes, and act all crazy. Who would willingly ingest something like that?

Mercy, mercy me, Grady thinks. *Ol' Marvin Gaye was*

right. Things most surely aren't what they used to be. And it ain't just the ecology.

Grady realizes that he's standing in the middle of his bedroom, daydreaming rather than taking action. Frowning, he creeps over to the window.

All of the units in the Pine Village Apartment Complex are built as split-level structures. The four apartments at the front of the building, where the parking lot is located, are actually above the four apartments at the rear of the building. The residents of apartments 5-D through 9-D have to park their cars out front and then walk down a small hillside to the rear of the building to access their front doors. As a result, while their living room and kitchen windows face out on a lovely stretch of woodland and a large yard, the windows in their bedrooms are set high in the wall, near the ceiling, and display window wells and the edge of the parking lot, rather than any picturesque scenery. Sometimes, when Grady has accidentally left the blinds open, he can see the upstairs neighbor's feet as they walk by, although never any higher than their ankles. A few times, Grady has tried to see up Mrs. Carlucci's dress, but his attempts have been frustratingly unsuccessful.

He raises up on his tiptoes and peeks out the blind, craning his neck to see. Grady frowns, unsure of what's happening. He glimpses dozens of bare feet and bare legs. Some of them are bloody. They're all converging on the front of the building, as if whoever the feet are attached to are pressing themselves against the windows and doors of the apartments above. The banging noises are louder now, and Grady hears glass shatter. Someone shouts. Their words are lost beneath another gunshot.

It is then that Grady decides this is definitely not a dream. Nor is it a flashback. This is happening. This is all very real. The whirlwind that consumed Detroit has returned.

Moving as fast as his arthritis will allow, Grady grabs his keys from atop the dresser and opens his underwear drawer. Inside, half hidden beneath ratty boxer shorts and faded, hole-ridden socks, is a locked steel pistol box. He pulls the box out and sets it on the dresser, noticing as he does that his hands are not shaking. He's scared, yes, but that old training is kicking in. Just like riding a bike.

He grimaces as a burp, sour and acidic and tasting of fear, bubbles up inside him.

Grady uses his key to unlock the box, pulls out his Smith & Wesson .38 revolver, loads it, and then makes his way to the kitchen. He tries the phone, intent on calling 911, but there's no dial tone. He clicks the receiver a few times, but is only met with more silence.

Hanging up the phone, Grady glances down at his shoes, which are lined up against the alcove wall between the kitchen and the living room, next to the front door. He hesitates, feeling a tightness in his chest. His breath hitches, and he becomes aware that he's sweating. He readjusts his grip on the pistol, waiting for the pain in his chest to subside. Eventually, it starts to, albeit slowly.

Grady glances at the front door, making sure it's locked. Then his gaze returns to his shoes. He debates what to do next. If he were a younger man, there would be no question. He'd go outside and help whoever is in trouble. But he is not a younger man, and he's not going to help anybody if he has a heart attack in the parking lot or has to defend somebody and can't get off a shot fast enough because his arthritic fingers won't squeeze the trigger fast enough.

His heart is still beating fast, but the pain is gone now. He moves to the living room window, parts the blinds, and peeks outside. His eyes widen in surprise. There are perhaps two dozen naked people running across the yard toward the building. Between them and his front door is a short young man with brownish-blond hair and glasses. Squinting, Grady recognizes him as Adam Love. He and his fiancée share an apartment together in the C-building. Grady knows them because their dog got loose last year and ended up at Grady's apartment door. Since then, the two younger people always wave at him in passing, or make small talk with him if their paths happen to cross, usually at the garbage dumpsters or the complex's laundromat. Last winter, when there was nine inches of snow on the ground and Grady's arthritis was particularly bad, Adam had been kind enough to shovel Grady's sidewalk for him (because if the tenants waited for Pine Village's management to clear the snow, they'd have to wait for Spring).

Adam's expression is terrified, and his forehead is bloody. He glances behind him as he runs, stumbles, and then falls sprawling onto the grass. The naked people charge toward him, waving a variety of weapons.

"Get up!" Grady slams his fist against the window, shaking the blinds. "Get up, goddamn it!"

Adam struggles to his feet, but he seems disoriented. As he wipes the blood from his forehead, his pursuers close the gap between them and him. Adam doesn't notice. Instead, he stares at the blood on his hand.

Cursing, Grady unlocks the door and steps outside.

Seven

The Exit:
Apartment 7-D

As the Exit, Javier Mendez has killed one-hundred and thirty-seven people over the last fifteen years, but it's not something he enjoys doing. He reads what the newspapers and the serial killer websites say about him—all the reasons and speculation they give for why he does what he does—and all of them are wrong. Wrong about his possible identity (they think he's a white man in his thirties), wrong about his motives (they say it's everything from rage at the modern world to an abusive childhood), and wrong about his psyche (that he's a sociopath who is driven by an uncontrollable urge to kill). He only kills when he has to. It is something he avoids doing unless absolutely necessary.

Which is why he doesn't start running over the naked people with his car until they attack him.

He has just gotten home after a six-hour round-trip drive to Rockaway, New Jersey, where he was closing a doorway before one of the entities from the place outside the universe broke through. The spaces between realities are full of such creatures. They travel a path beyond space and time, looking for an entrance into the world, and their attempted breaches are happening more and more often. That's why his work is more important than ever before, and that is why he can't allow himself to be caught. It's also the reason he gets so annoyed with the press and the internet experts who claim to understand his motivations. They understand nothing. He is an exit. He closes doorways before they open. He knows all-too-well what will happen if he doesn't, because he's seen it in his dreams. Those nightmares always begin the same way—with him not closing a doorway in time, and then one of the entities gains access to the world. In one dream, a living darkness engulfs the planet, devouring anything with a spark of life—people, animals, even the plants. In another dream, most of the world is flooded after a terrible deluge, and giant worms and other bizarre monstrosities slaughter the survivors. In yet another nightmare, the dead come back to life as zombies and hunt humanity into extinction. In another, there's a war between the zombies and some sort of bizarre ocean monsters that looks like a cross between a crab and a scorpion and a lobster.

The vast majority of these attempted breaches occur in the Mid-Atlantic region of the United States. The general populace remain blissfully unaware of them, but not so the Exit. He knows all about them, and what's more, he knows why they're happening. The culprit is the Interstate Highway System. With a total length of forty-seven thousand, seven hundred and fourteen miles, it is the second longest highway system in the world, exceeded only by one in China. As originally designed, it was supposed to be in the shape of an ancient and extremely complex magical glyph, but that never happened because two of the original interstates, I-95 and I-70, have missing interchanges that were never completed. Because the highway system—and thus the glyph—isn't contiguous, the walls of reality are thin in the Mid-Atlantic region.

And that is why the Exit kills. It has nothing to do with his childhood or his mental health. He kills because sealing off a breach and turning an entrance into an exit requires a sacrifice. Whenever he senses that a breach is about to occur anywhere in Pennsylvania, Maryland, New Jersey, Delaware, Virginia, or West Virginia, he goes there to stop it, and the only way to prevent something like that from happening is with blood. He kills because he has to. He kills because it was the only way to save the lives of everyone else. He kills because it is his job.

He's not crazy. If he was crazy then his stomach wouldn't be churning right now, and he wouldn't be so short of breath, as his tires crunch over a naked man who, only seconds ago, had been swinging a sledgehammer at the hood of his car.

He'd first noticed something was wrong upon exiting Interstate 83 and taking the ramp onto Route 30 in York. Dozens of emergency vehicles rushed past, on their way to elsewhere. Then, he'd spotted several fires—two residences engulfed in flames and a fire burning at the old Caterpillar plant. Finally, while driving along Route 24 through Manchester, he'd spotted a woman standing along the side of the road, clutching a knife and staring intently at the passing traffic. But, unlike the people here in the parking lot of the Pine Village Apartment Complex, she hadn't been naked.

He had avoided checking his phone, because he was a stickler about not getting pulled over and not causing an accident. Stupidity led to being caught, and being caught wasn't something that he—or the world—could afford. He'd tried the local radio stations, but all of them were playing prerecorded, syndicated shows, except for WSBA, which curiously, seemed to be off the air. But as more police cars rushed past him, he'd wondered if there were even any units available for speed traps and traffic control tonight.

He made it home without further incident. Then, as he'd pulled into the parking lot at the complex, looking forward to curling up on the couch in his apartment and perhaps reading a book for a little while before bed, he'd seen the mob—dozens and dozens of crazed, nude people swarming the grounds and attacking the residents of the complex. They kicked in doors and crawled through broken windows, and carried a bizarre array of weaponry. They kicked, clubbed, and hacked a man lying on the sidewalk, and held a woman in place while another among their ranks slammed the dumpster door against her head over and over again.

They shot a wailing child and stabbed a fleeing teenager. They glared, snarled, and sneered at him, illuminated in his headlights as he slowed to a halt.

The Exit paused, running through his options as the mob converged toward him, acting almost as one. His knife and the rest of his tools were in the trunk, so the Exit used the only weapon he had available. Easing his foot off the brake, he pressed the accelerator and slammed into the crowd.

Now, he's made it halfway across the complex, just passing by Building C, and the crowd hasn't lessened. If anything, there seem to be more of them. One of the naked people bludgeons his driver's side door with a fire extinguisher while another knocks out one of his headlights with a rock. The car shakes and rattles, being struck from all sides, but he keeps his foot on the gas, knowing that if he stops now, he'll be dead. He swerves and veers, clipping as many of them as he can while simultaneously trying not to run over a large mass of attackers, lest he get stuck.

He bears down on a man with a gun looming in his lone headlight. The man looks like a bodybuilder, all six-pack abs and swollen bulges, and his naked skin shines with sweat. He raises the gun as the Exit plows into him. There's a flash and then a boom, but the gun is pointed upward as the weightlifter disappears beneath the front bumper. The car bounces up and down, the shocks groaning in protest, and then begins to shudder as the man gets caught on the undercarriage. The Exit gives it more gas and glances in the rearview mirror long enough to see the wet, red stain he's leaving in the car's wake. Worse is the sound the body makes as it is scraped along the pavement. He can hear it even though the windows are closed and the people outside are howling. He doesn't think he's ever heard a more horrendous sound. It reminds him of wet Velcro.

As he reaches Building D, he spots a large group of assailants trying to break into apartment 1-D—where the writer lives. More naked figures fill the parking lot. Several of them are clustered around the clothed body of a young man lying next to a U-Haul truck. As the Exit runs down a woman armed with a baseball bat, he sees a young girl of about seven or eight years of age pick up the corpse's severed right arm. Raising it over her head, she laughs gleefully, and then runs toward the car, as if intending to bash in his windshield with the grisly appendage.

The Exit spins the steering wheel, knocking her over with the front bumper, and then swerves to avoid another oncoming cluster of attackers. He realizes he needs to think quickly. The parking lot ends just beyond his building, terminating into woodlands and an alleyway to the right. The alley is unreachable because there are trees and saplings between it and the parking lot. He fights to stay calm, but feels the panic welling up inside of him. The roof buckles as someone clambers onto the top of the car.

"That won't do."

He cranks the wheel hard to the left, and the car shimmies as what is left of the bodybuilder's corpse slides out from underneath it. He sees a naked teenaged boy tumble off the side of the car, arms flailing. The kid's arm snaps as he hits the pavement. Then, the Exit aims for the hillside. There is just enough room for his car to fit between the stairs and Building C. He is glad the weightlifter isn't there anymore, because he feels the undercarriage rubbing against the grass. He glances to his right at the crowd breaking into the apartment, and one particular individual catches his attention. Standing behind the others is the most obese man the Exit has ever seen— so overweight that he almost seems like a caricature, as if his girth were the result of Hollywood special effects. The man's face is split in a wide, garish grin, and his head tilts back and forth—tick, tock, tick, tock. The effect is almost mesmerizing.

Then, the car is barreling down the hill and the man vanishes from sight, and the Exit turns his attention back to the windshield and shouts in surprise.

He hits the bottom of the hill with such force that his chest is driven into the steering wheel. The pain is immense, almost blinding. Gasping for breath, the Exit struggles to keep the car moving. It seems to want to go in all four directions at once. It careens to the right, narrowly missing the bottom of the cement stairs. The tires dig furrows into the grass.

The backyard is also filled with naked people, but there are not nearly as many as there are in the parking lot above. The Exit debates his choices. His apartment is three doors down. He can park in front of it, using the car as a partial blockade, and try to get inside before the hordes can reach him. Or, he can continue across the yard, swerving around the forest to the rear of the property and heading back out toward the entrance to the apartment complex. The only problem with that second choice is that he'll have to drive through a fairly deep culvert, and also weave around the garbage dumpsters.

There are angry, guttural shouts behind him as many of his attackers scurry down the hill and stairs. One of them trips and falls, and disappears beneath the feet of his onrushing companions. None of the crowd stops, or seems to show the least bit of concern.

The Exit is about to try for his apartment when he is presented with a third choice, as further out in the yard, he spots two of his neighbors—old Mr. Hicks from next door and a young man who lives in Building C—about to be set upon by a pack of opponents. Gripping the steering wheel, he stomps the accelerator and speeds toward them. The tires spray grass and dirt and rocks on his pursuers.

They do not slow down.

He doesn't slow down either.

Eight

Phil and Beth: Apartment 8-D

"Maybe we should go out there," Phil says again, listening to the sounds of chaos all around the complex. "Just take a quick look and see what's happening."

"Are you crazy?" Beth is staring at her cell phone, trying to make a call. "Do you hear that?"

"Yeah, I hear it. That's why I'm thinking I should check it out. What if somebody is shooting up the complex?"

"What do the police say every time that happens?"

"To shelter in place?"

"Right! Shelter in place." Beth turns her attention back to the phone. "We need to stay inside. Whoever it is has guns. We should stay away from the doors and windows and…"

She trails off. The phone shakes in her hands.

"Who are you calling?" Phil asks.

"My Mom."

Phil blinks twice before responding. "Beth, what's your Mom going to do?"

"I don't know, Phil! But I'm scared and I want my mother and don't you dare go outside and leave me in here by myself! Just don't…"

Sighing, Phil walks back down the hallway, where Beth is crouched with her back against the wall. He reaches out and strokes her hair. Then he kneels beside her, looking his wife in the eye.

"Baby, listen. I know you're scared. Truth is, I'm scared, too. But think about it for a minute. I mean logically. What's your Mom going to do? Even if she came down here, what's to say she wouldn't be in danger, just like everybody else?"

"I don't know."

"And I don't either. But save the battery on your phone. We don't know what's happening. Better to stay prepared."

Blinking, Beth wipes tears from her eyes. "It doesn't matter anyway. I can't get a signal. What if she's worried about us? If this is on the news already, she might try to call me and make sure we're okay."

"I'm sure she's fine. And even if she does try to get here, they're not going to let her through."

"Do you think so?"

Phil nods. "Sure. I'll bet they've got a police cordon up around the whole complex. Nobody in or out except emergency personnel. It's not like somebody is shooting up all of Central Pennsylvania. Whatever is happening out there, it's only happening right here."

"How do you know?"

"Because that's crazy."

"Not if it was terrorists."

"Terrorists attacking here? Come on, hon. I know you're scared, but we can't start overreacting. We need to keep our shit together."

Beth shrugs. "Yeah…"

"It's like you said. We should stay here and shelter in place. You were right."

Beth smiles. "Say that again."

"You were right."

"I never get tired of hearing that."

"Some women prefer hearing 'I love you' instead."

"I'm not some women."

Phil slides his arms around Beth and pulls her close, smelling her shampoo. Her soft hair tickles his nose.

"I hate this place," she whispers.

"I know. Me, too."

Phil and Beth are both twenty-seven years old. They

met at college, and have been married for a year. They live in the Pine Village Apartment Complex because the rent is cheap, and they're saving up to have enough money for a down payment on a house. Neither of them like it here. The apartment is small and cramped, and bugs keep seeming to find their way inside. Beth doesn't mind the insects but Phil is deathly afraid of them. Bugs have always been his phobia, ever since he was a kid. When they first moved in, the place stank like cat piss. In the time they've lived here, the smell has abated, for the most part, but they still catch it on their clothes sometimes, and in the carpet. Beth likes to joke that they should just get a cat, but they can't, because Phil is allergic.

And so, here they stay, squirreling away their savings, and talking of how awesome it will be when they finally move out. Beth's father has repeatedly offered to lend them the money, but Phil always declines, insisting that they want to do it themselves. The realtors have told them they need about twenty or thirty thousand dollars for the type of home they're looking for. Phil works in IT for the cable company, and Beth has a job in the billing department of a health insurance company. At night, they take turns making dinner. Then they cuddle on the couch they received as a wedding present and watch Netflix. They make love two or three times a week. They still have things to talk about when they aren't. The apartment isn't so bad in those moments.

But they still save their money and they still look at homes for sale online, and dream of the day they can buy one.

Beth stirs. "You made sure the door was locked, right?"

"Yeah." Phil nods. "Do you think we should barricade it somehow? Maybe put something over the windows?"

"It might not be a bad idea. And we should keep the lights turned off, too. Maybe they'll think we aren't home."

"That's a good idea. I'll—"

Outside, a car horn blares, interrupting him. They hear an engine thrumming loud enough that the walls seem to vibrate. Headlights flash in the living room window, which is weird, since that window faces the backyard. It's just grass and sidewalk out there—no place for a car to drive. Luckily, the blinds are closed, so the glare is somewhat muted.

Phil frowns. "What the hell?"

"Maybe it's the police. Maybe they rolled up into the yard?"

"Let's hope so!"

Beth puts a finger to his lips. "Don't yell. We don't want whoever it is to know we're in here."

"I'm not yelling."

"Yes, you are."

"I'm not yelling, Beth. I'm just trying to be heard over that damn car! What the hell has gotten into you?"

Beth flinches, and then Phil does, too. When they first got engaged, Phil's father gave them the advice of 'never go to bed angry with each other.' So far, that advice has worked. They have never had a fight or argument, and have never raised their voices in anger at one another. Both of them are aware that they seem to be now, driven by fear and uncertainty and paranoia. After a moment, Beth says what's on both their minds.

"I don't want to fight. I'm scared. You're scared. Let's just stick together, okay?"

Smiling, Phil nods. "I'm sorry, hon."

"I'm sorry, too."

The sub-woofer on their surround sound system pops as the power suddenly shuts off. The digital clock goes blank. In the kitchen, the refrigerator's compressor falls silent. Outside, the horn continues to blare, drowning out the screams and the gunshots.

"The power's out," Phil says.

Beth nods. "I'm really getting scared, Phil. This is bad."

"Maybe that car out there hit a pole or something."

"There aren't any electrical poles in the yard."

"Listen," Phil speaks slowly, trying to sound reassuring. "I want to take a peek out the window."

Beth stiffens, and her eyes go wide. Before she can speak, Phil pushes ahead.

"Just a quick glance. That's all. We need to know what's going on. How else are we going to protect ourselves? Nobody is going to see me. I'm just going to look through the blinds and then come right back here."

Beth shrugs. "Okay. You're right. Just be careful."

Phil gets to his feet, grinning. "You know me."

"That's why I said to be careful."

Crouching low, Phil makes his way down the hall. The glare from the headlights gets brighter as he nears the window, creeping through the spaces between the blinds. If they were open, he probably wouldn't be able to see anything right now. As it is, he has to shield his eyes with his hand as he parts the blinds and peeks outside.

"What do you see?" Beth calls. "What is it?"

"It's Mister Hicks and Mister Mendez and…some guy I don't know. And there's…"

He trails off, gaping out the window.

"There's what? What do you see, Phil? What's going on?"

"There's naked people."

"What?"

"There's a bunch of naked people." He lets the blinds fall shut and walks back down the hall. His complexion turns chalk white. "And I think they're going to kill our neighbors."

"What do you mean naked?"

Phil starts to respond, but then he bursts into tears. He stands there, shaking and in shock. Terrified, Beth rushes to him and pulls him close.

The car horn stops suddenly. When it does, they notice that the screams and gunshots and other sounds have ceased, as well. The silence is even more terrifying than the chaos that preceded it.

Night arrives, and engulfs the Pine Village Apartment Complex in darkness.

PART TWO

BLOCK
PARTY

Nine

Sam, Terri, Caleb, Stephanie, Mrs. Carlucci, Shaggy, and Turo: Apartment 1-D

The irony is not lost on Sam. Only a few short minutes ago, he was just about to kill himself. Now, plans of suicide have been put on hold and instead, he's fighting to stay alive. He doesn't pause to consider why, because there's no time for self-reflection. Four of the cheap pressboard bookshelves are pressed up against the broken living room windows, forming a double-layered barricade. The sofa and another bookshelf have been shoved against the locked front door. In the kitchen, the refrigerator blocks half of the window. The window's other half is covered by the small upended kitchen table—a furnishing Sam has never used because he always eats his solitary meals in front of the television or his computer. The table is propped in place by a microwave cart. Atop the microwave is a jumble of debris—the coffee pot, pans, books—anything that could help form a barrier. Sam is pretty sure this area will be the weakest link.

He snaps his fingers at the tall, scraggly kid with the gun. Sam doesn't know his name. He only knows that the guy lives in the apartment below him, along with his short friend. Both of them are currently staring at the door, wide-eyed and dazed. Sam is pretty sure they're stoned. He wishes he was, as well.

When the guy doesn't notice, Sam snaps his fingers at him again. "Hey, what's your name?"

"Me? Shaggy."

Sam suppresses a laugh, resisting the urge to shout, "Zoinks, Scoob!" He knows this reaction is driven by panic and shock, but that doesn't make it any less amusing.

"Okay, Shaggy." He nods at the gun in the kid's hand.

"You got more ammo for that thing?"

Shaggy glances down at his weapon as if he'd forgotten it. "Yeah. The magazine's full and I got another in my pocket. All fucking hollow points."

"Okay, good. I want you at that kitchen window. That's our weakest defense, so you need to be ready to pick them off if they get through. Your buddy can help. What's your name?"

"T-turo."

"Okay, Turo. I've got kitchen knives in a holder on the counter. Steak knives and such. You can grab one of those."

"The fuck am I gonna do with a steak knife?"

"Stab anyone reaching through the window. Just make sure you stay clear so Shaggy doesn't shoot you by mistake. You guys got this?"

Nodding, Shaggy grabs Turo by the arm and directs him toward the kitchen.

"Come on, dude."

Turo follows along as if half asleep.

Sam turns to Mrs. Carlucci, who is staring intently at the door. Behind her are their new neighbors, a pretty young red-haired woman and her little boy. Both of them appear as terrified as Sam feels. The boy clings to his mother's side, and she in turn, has one arm tightly wrapped around him, holding him close. Stephanie stands behind them, seemingly in a daze. She has the same blank expression as Shaggy's roommate. Moments ago, Sam saw her stab and slash several attackers with a butcher knife. She's still holding the knife now, but seems unaware of it. Indeed, she doesn't seem aware of anything. Her eyes are glassy, and her posture is slack.

"Stephanie, are you okay?"

She doesn't answer. Doesn't even look at him.

"Stephanie? Are you hurt?"

Outside, the chainsaw roars again. Seconds later, there

is a terrible screeching noise as the chainsaw's owner tries it against Sam's front door. Everyone except Mrs. Carlucci screams. Sam's scream is the loudest.

"These doors aren't made out of wood," Mrs. Carlucci shouts. "They'll hold."

"What the fuck are they made out of then?" Shaggy yells from the kitchen.

"Watch your language and don't be fresh! I don't know what they're made of. Plastic? Vinyl? But it's not wood. I tried to drive a nail through one, to hang up my Christmas wreath one year. The nail kept bending."

"Mrs. Carlucci, you keep an eye on that over there," Sam suggests, pointing at the living room window. "Stephanie, can you help her?"

Stephanie blinks, as if waking from a dream, and turns her head to Sam. "The fat one had a Hello Kitty tattoo."

"What?" Sam frowns. "Are you okay, hon? Did they hurt you?"

"The fat one," she explains. "Outside. The one with the twitchy head. He had a tattoo. That's the last thing I remember. After that I sort of…blacked out. What's happening?"

"I think you're in shock," Sam says, and squeezes her arm in what he hopes is a reassuring gesture. "They're trying to get inside. We've got to hold them off until the cops get here. Think you can help Mrs. Carlucci guard those windows?"

"Yes," Stephanie agrees. "I can do that. I'm sorry…"

"Don't be sorry. I'm scared shitless, Steph."

She tilts her head to the side, smiling slowly. "You're the first person to call me Steph, Sam. Until now, it's been Stephanie."

"Oh yeah?" He grins. "Do you like it?"

"I don't know. It's…different."

"Well, let's make it through this alive and then you can decide. Fair enough?"

She nods, still smiling. "Sounds like a plan."

The chainsaw scores against the door again. Stephanie flinches, but retains her composure and control. Sam jumps so hard he nearly drops his gun. The little boy buries his face in his mother's thigh, and Sam notices that she's squeezing him so hard her knuckles have turned white.

"I'm Sam," he says. "You're the new neighbor?"

The redhead looks at him as if he just asked her if she'd like a rabid weasel. Her pupils remind him of perfectly round circles of black ink. Her upper lip quivers, and her cheeks are wet.

"It's going to be okay," he says. "The barricades will hold. Can you do me a favor?"

The new neighbor nods, but when she opens her mouth to speak, she only whimpers.

"Can you and your son...I'm assuming he's your son?"

She nods again, a bit more emphatically.

"Okay. Can you take him into the bedrooms and check the windows back there?"

"But...they might be outside."

"They might," Sam agrees, raising his voice as the chainsaw attack is renewed on the door. "But those windows are way up off the ground. It's a twelve foot drop. Basically, I just want you to close the blinds and curtains, and see if the back yard is clear. Maybe we can get out that way, somehow."

He pauses, lets his gaze drop down to the terrified little boy, and then back up to hers.

"Plus, it's probably quieter back there."

Something slams against the front door, and this time, they all jump. Glass shatters in the kitchen.

"They're coming," Shaggy yells. "Heads up!"

"Go on," Sam tells her. "Take him in the back. We've got this."

Biting her lip, the redhead blinks back tears. Then she

gently pries her son from her side and guides him down the hallway.

"Come on, Caleb," she says. "It's going to be okay."

Sam turns his attention back to the front of the apartment. The door shudders again in its frame as something heavy batters against it on the outside. Judging by the sound, Sam suspects it is the fat man. The sound of the idling chainsaw shifts, moving toward the living room windows. A moment later, it begins to rev again. More glass breaks in the kitchen. A gunshot thunders through the apartment.

"They're trying to get through the kitchen," Shaggy hollers.

"Hold them off," Sam responds.

"Fuck you, motherfucker. Get in here and fucking help us!"

The bookshelves in front of the living room windows vibrate and tremble. Then the chainsaw chews through them, sending splinters of pressboard and plywood flying into the air. Mrs. Carlucci raises her weapon to fire.

"No," Sam calls. "Don't waste your bullets! Just wait."

"But they'll get through."

"Wait until you see them. Otherwise, you're going to waste your ammo."

The door groans on its hinges, and the chainsaw bursts through another section of bookshelves. The smell of gasoline and oil fills the living room. In the kitchen, pots and pans crash to the floor with a clatter. Then two more gunshots ring out.

"You got him," Shaggy's roommate shouts.

"Push that fucking microwave back in place," Shaggy says.

Another blow rains down on the door. This time, the force of it sends the bookshelves in front of it toppling to the floor. Sam jumps back, narrowly avoiding them. The light fixture in the ceiling swings back and forth. At the same time, the chainsaw makes another thrust, splintering the barrier in front of the windows. A naked mob swarm against the broken panes, reaching through, and pushing what remains of the blockade out of the way.

Mrs. Carlucci raises her gun again and fires, squeezing off two shots directly into the crowd. Both rounds find their targets, but the attackers' screams of pain are lost beneath the cacophony of rage. More blows batter the door in rapid succession.

"I'm empty," Mrs. Carlucci yells, backing away from the window.

"You only fired two fucking rounds," Shaggy says.

"I fired the rest outside," the old woman explains, "and I told you to watch your mouth!"

Sam tries to respond to them but finds himself speechless. His heart pounds in his chest, and his ears are ringing.

Screaming, Stephanie rushes forward and slashes at the cluster of grasping arms, hacking and slicing through fingers and palms and forearms. The crowd recoils, yanking their arms back through the broken windows, cutting them more. Sam's splintered bookshelves and windowsill are splattered with blood, chunks of fake wood, and broken glass.

"We need help in here," Shaggy pleads. His voice sounds frantic. "Somebody?"

"I'm empty," Mrs. Carlucci repeats.

"What is that?" Sam asks, panting as the door vibrates in its frame again.

"What's what?"

"Your gun. What caliber?"

"My husband's forty-five."

"I don't have any ammo for it." He holds up his gun. "I've only got this."

"Then you'd better point me toward those kitchen

knives." She crosses the living room, heading for the kitchen.

"Help," Shaggy yells.

"Hold your horses," Mrs. Carlucci responds. "I'm coming."

"That door isn't going to hold," Sam tells Stephanie. "Can you stand watch while I check the bedrooms for something else to bolster it?"

She salutes him with the knife. "Don't take too long."

"That's the idea. Just hold them off."

As he turns away, Sam hears Mrs. Carlucci in the kitchen, hollering at Shaggy and his friend to get out of her way.

Sam hurries down the hall. His bedroom is dark. He fumbles for the light switch on the wall, but when he flicks it, nothing happens.

"The power is out," the young mother tells him.

As his eyes adjust to the darkness, he spots her sitting on his bed. Her son is curled up with his head in her lap. She's stroking the boy's hair, trying to soothe him.

"I'm Terri," she says. "You're Sam, I think I heard them say?"

"That's right. Sam Miller. I'd say it's nice to meet you, but under the circumstances…"

"Yeah."

Sam hears the pounding on the door getting louder again. Shaggy fires another round. Sam is grateful that he's taking his time, and saving his bullets, rather than simply emptying the magazine. He might be a stoner, but the kid can obviously keep a cool head under pressure. Sam hurries to the dresser and opens the top drawer. Then he feels around and begins filling his pants pockets with spare ammunition.

"There are more crazies in the backyard," Terri says, "and somebody in a car. But I don't think the driver is one of them."

"A car?"

Sam moves over to the window and peers outside. Sure enough, he sees a car—one he recognizes as belonging to the man in apartment 7-D—running over naked people. He also spots the neighbor from apartment 6-D and another, younger man, both of whom are fleeing toward the building.

"Sam," Stephanie calls, "better hurry!"

"Coming!" Sam kneels next to the bed. "What's your name, buddy?"

Stirring, the boy looks him in the eye.

"I'm Caleb," he mumbles.

"Caleb, I'm Sam. I want you to know that it's okay to be scared. I'm scared, too. You wouldn't believe how scared I am. But right now, I need you to help me with something. You think you can do that?"

Caleb sits up slowly. "What?"

"Help me empty out that dresser over there so your mom and I can haul it into the living room."

"Okay." Caleb glances up at his mother.

"Come on," Terri says, standing up. "Let's hurry, though."

"Sam," Stephanie shouts again, "the door's not going to hold much longer!"

"Just a second!" He yanks out the top drawer and dumps his underwear and socks on the floor.

Grinning, Caleb does the same with a second drawer, depositing a pile of t-shirts at his feet. Sam and Terri make quick work of the remaining drawers. Sam shoves the Taurus in his waistband and tilts the dresser back toward him. He nods at Terri.

"Grab the bottom."

The dresser is made from the same cheap materials as the bookshelves, so it isn't heavy. This makes it easy to carry, but Sam isn't sure it will do anything to help secure the front door. He realizes he isn't thinking clearly. He shouldn't have bothered emptying the drawers. The extra weight would have helped. He's letting panic drive him, rather than logic. They reach the living room, and he's about to voice his concern regarding the dresser's weight, when he realizes that it no longer matters.

The lock snaps with an audible pop and the door bursts open, dangling on one hinge. The fat man fills the doorway, grinning and drooling as his head tilts from side to side. In his hands are the bloodied remains of a partial corpse, missing its arms, one leg, and part of its head. The portion of its head that remains has been squashed like an overripe melon. With dawning horror, Sam understands what's been banging on his door. The fat man has been using the corpse as a makeshift battering ram. Now, he tries to squeeze his greasy bulk through the doorway. His rolls of fat fold and crease, and the door leans crookedly on its one remaining hinge. Sam gags. The stench wafting off of the fat man is revolting.

Terri drops her end of the dresser and shrieks, "Randy!"

It takes Sam a second to realize that she's referring to the corpse. How she recognizes it is beyond him, but apparently she does.

Caleb turns and flees back into the bedroom. In the kitchen, Shaggy unleashes another volley of gunshots as, judging by the sounds, the mob begins trying to breach the windows again. Mrs. Carlucci shouts something unintelligible. Terri stares in horror at the grisly monstrosity looming in the doorway. Sam gapes dumbly, as well, arms straining as he continues to hold up his end of the dresser. Only Stephanie acts, rushing forward, butcher knife raised over her head to deliver a deadly strike. The fat man's eyes dart toward her, and then he flings the corpse in her direction. The bloodied meat slams into her, knocking Stephanie to the floor. She shouts as the knife slips from her grasp and tumbles across the carpet.

The fat man squirms and struggles, trying to force his way inside, but he's too wide to fit through the narrow doorway.

Behind him, the other crazies gibber and snarl. Their words aren't any sort of language. It's a rabid, maniacal sound.

Stephanie writhes beneath the leaking dead man, choking with disgust. Sam is about to help her, when he spies the fat man receding from the door. The space is open for a second, and then the horde surges forward. There are so many of them that they block each other from getting inside. They begin to fight amongst themselves, scratching and punching one another. Shouting, Sam drags the dresser toward the doorway and shoves it into the space. The assailants push and claw at it. Sam pushes back, locking his knees and planting his feet. Fingernails claw furrows in the skin on the back of his hands. A naked woman clambers over the top, so thin she looks cadaverous, and swipes at his eyes. Sam reels back, and the woman springs to the floor. She grins, flashing receding gums with missing teeth. Sam fumbles, trying to free his pistol from his waistband, as the woman lunges.

Then, Mrs. Carlucci appears beside him, armed with an aerosol can full of oven cleaner. She sprays it in the attacker's eyes, and the naked woman falls to the floor, shrieking in agony, and clawing at her face. Mrs. Carlucci kicks her in the ribs and steps forward, unleashing a stream of toxic chemicals at the rest of the mob. They scream and cry, frothing with rage, and recoil from the doorway. Mrs. Carlucci presses on, leaning over the dresser and extending her arm, spraying back and forth.

Sam hears someone else screaming, and realizes that it's Stephanie. He notices that she's managed to retrieve her knife. Now she's on top of the naked woman, who's coiled beneath her, blinded and flailing as Stephanie plunges the butcher knife into her again and again. Blood splashes them both in wide arcs, splattering the walls and carpet. Stephanie's arm moves like a machine, stabbing and slashing, even after the naked woman stops moving.

The mob rushes the open door again, as Shaggy and Turo run out of the kitchen.

"They're getting through," Shaggy pants, wild-eyed. "We can't hold them back anymore. There are too many!"

"You've got a gun," Sam shouts. "Shoot them!"

"For every fucking one I shoot, two more take their fucking place."

He wheels, fires four shots into the crowd at the door, and then pushes past Sam and flees down the hallway toward the bedrooms. Mrs. Carlucci sends another arc of oven cleaner at the horde, but then the stream sputters and dies.

"I'm empty again."

She tosses the can at the crowd. It bounces off a naked man's forehead. Then she follows Shaggy and Turo.

Sam stares at the mob. He glances down and sees a long-handled axe lying in the doorway, apparently dropped by one of the people Mrs. Carlucci blinded. He bends down to grab it, and hears the blockade in the kitchen crash to the floor.

"Shit." He seizes the axe. Its weight feels reassuring. "Stephanie, come on!"

She looks up at him, her face drenched in blood. Her chest heaves. "I killed someone…"

"You had no choice. Come on. We've got to go."

She rises unsteadily to her feet. Sam grabs her hand and leads her toward the bedroom. Their footfalls echo down the hall. Behind them, the dresser creaks as the mob pushes it out of the way. The last hinge snaps and the front door crashes to the floor. Something that sounds like a stampeding herd of cows trumpets out of the kitchen.

"Don't look back," Sam shouts, pulling Stephanie along. "Just run!"

At the end of the hallway, he spies Shaggy standing in the bedroom doorway, gun raised. Sam flinches.

"Don't shoot us, you asshole!"

Shaggy motions with the gun. "Then hurry the fuck up!"

Shaggy moves aside as they reach him. Sam shoves Stephanie into the bedroom and then turns to look. His eyes widen in horror.

"Oh shit!"

The crazies rush into the apartment. Shaggy empties his magazine, firing into their midst. Sam has to admit, the stoner is a great shot. Each bullet finds a target, and each target drops to the floor. More naked attackers clamber over their fallen comrades. Shaggy pushes past Sam.

"Dude," he shouts, "come on!"

Still hefting the axe, Sam slams the bedroom door shut behind him as the mob pours into the living room and down the hallway. Their pounding feet drown out everything, including his scream.

Ten

Grady, The Exit, Adam, Phil, and Beth: The Yard

As the crowd of naked people begins to surround them again, Grady fires two rounds. The gun jumps in his hands, and the bullets miss. He takes a deep breath and forces himself to remain still. Then he squeezes the trigger four more times in quick succession. This time, all four rounds hit their intended targets. Three of the crazies drop. The other one staggers backward, hand clasped to a sucking chest wound. The rest of the mob barely seems to notice. Grady is not surprised by their reaction. Obviously, there's something very wrong with these people, given their current state of agitation. But even if they were normal, they might not notice that he's just shot four of them, since Mendez from next door just ran over three times that number with his car, crushing them beneath his wheels and buying Grady and Adam a brief moment of respite. Now the car is racing across the yard, away from them. Some of the horde give chase, further lessening the numbers he and Adam face.

Grady reloads on the run, arthritic fingers fumbling with the bullets. The task is made even more difficult by the fact that he can't seem to stop shaking. He hasn't been this scared since Vietnam. The pain in his chest returns, more pronounced this time. Grady winces when he draws breath. Adam stumbles along next to him, still disoriented and half-blind as more blood streams down his forehead into his eyes. His skin is very pale, and his pupils are dilated. He keeps glancing back at their pursuers, and each time he does, he slows down.

"Where's your fiancée?" Grady asks, trying to keep the

younger man focused as they flee. He feels bad for not being able to remember the girl's name in the heat of the moment.

Adam shakes his head. "They…there was a knock on the door and she…"

He falters, and then, sobbing, begins to turn back toward the crowd. Grady grabs his arm and pulls.

"Come on, Adam. Focus. Head for my front door."

"But they…they had knives…and a piece of rebar. They…"

"It's okay. It's going to be okay."

"No, it's not. She's dead!"

"I'm sorry, Adam. I—"

A naked man who Grady recognizes as a tenant of Building B charges ahead of the rest of the crowd. He's carrying a broken mop handle, the tip of which is stained brown with blood. Grady pauses and shoots him in the head. The man runs four more steps before tumbling over. He never lets go of the mop handle.

"Mr. Hicks! Mr. Hicks, wait up!"

It takes Grady a second to find the speaker. The voice comes from across the yard, near the apartment complex. He turns toward it, searching, and spots Phil and Beth, the newlyweds who live a few doors down from him, inching along the side of the building. Phil clutches an aluminum baseball bat. The crowd is between them and Grady, and don't seem to have noticed the young couple. That changes as Phil waves and shouts again.

"Mr. Hicks, we're coming. Wait up!"

"Wait up," Grady mutters. "That boy's crazy. Wait up my ass."

Mendez whips the car around in the yard, tires chewing up the grass and topsoil as the vehicle bares down on the crowd again. The engine chortles manically, and the mob's rear flank scatters. Mendez lays on the horn. Grady isn't sure if he does this to further distract and disorient their attackers, but if so, it doesn't achieve the desired results. Mendez doesn't get the main crowd's attention until he slams into them at full speed. Naked bodies fly and tumble like bowling pins. The car bounces up and down, and for one moment, Grady is sure his neighbor is going to crash. Then, Mendez regains control. The car's rear end fishtails, sliding on the grass, and he manages to clip two more pursuers. Then he roars off again across the yard. The naked people turn their attention back to Grady and Adam, but several of them splinter off from the main group and begin stalking toward Phil and Beth.

Struggling to stay upright, Grady guides Adam forward as the insane throng closes in on them again from three sides, herding them toward the apartment building. Grady realizes the crowd are doing the same thing to Phil and Beth. But in truth, there's nowhere else to run. He hears gunshots in the distance, over the mob's cries and Mendez's car. He realizes that whatever is happening here is taking place all across town.

"Head for my apartment," he shouts, realizing the newlyweds are already cut off from theirs.

Phil swings the bat, smashing an attacker in the face, pulping the man's lips and shattering his teeth. Phil uses it again to strike another pursuer in the stomach. The woman doubles over, immobilized. Beth claws and punches, fighting alongside her husband. She shrieks, and to Grady, she sounds both panicked and furious. He's heard men make that same noise, in the war. Now, the war is happening right here.

"I've got to get home," Adam mutters.

"Bullshit. You stick with me if you want to stay alive."

"But…"

A young boy, maybe ten or eleven years old, breaks free of the rest of the group and charges toward them. The kid clutches a broken glass bottle in one hand, and his lips are curled back in a snarl. Grady's attention is drawn to the braces on the boy's teeth. They seem strangely out of place. The boy closes the distance quickly, and Grady raises the Smith & Wesson, still staring at the orthodontics. He tries to aim, but his arms wobble. At the last minute, deciding he can't shoot the kid, no matter how murderous, he lets go of Adam's arm and sidesteps the young attacker, sticking out one foot and tripping the boy. The boy falls face first onto the grass. Grady winces when he hears the broken bottle being crushed beneath the kid's body.

Adam lopes away in a running, stumbling gait, heading back toward his building. Shouting his name, Grady steps over the fallen kid and reaches for him. That is a mistake. The boy rolls over and slashes at Grady's ankle with a shard of glass. Yelping, Grady teeters on one foot. Then, without thinking about it, he shoots the naked boy in the face. He realizes what he's done a split second after he pulls the trigger. Grady wants to take the action back, but it's too late. The boy's face implodes right between his nose and his left eye, collapsing into his head. Grady's stomach churns.

Phil shouts something—Grady can't understand him. He glances up and sees the two newlyweds still fighting off the frenzied attackers. Then, even though he doesn't want to look, his eyes are drawn back down to the dead boy. Grady notices that his shoes are spattered with the child's blood. The kid's brains cling to the blades of grass like chunks of red and gray cottage cheese.

"I'm sorry," Grady sobs, and he is.

Feeling his sock turn wet with blood, he limps after Adam, feebly gesturing for him to come back. Grady shouts, but if the younger man hears him, he doesn't turn around. Instead, Adam weaves back and forth in a sort of Z-formation, keeping his gaze fixed on Building-C. As a result, he doesn't see the mob rushing toward him until it is too late. Grady watches in horror as they quickly overwhelm him, dragging Adam to the ground and delivering countless vicious blows with fists and feet and various weapons. There are bricks and rocks and a hockey stick, and all of them are quickly slicked with blood. Adam's screams are horrific.

Shuddering, Grady raises the pistol, unsure of how many shots he has left. He takes aim, then hears someone growling behind him. He turns and sees a dozen more naked people closing in. Instead of helping Adam, Grady heads for his apartment again, leaving a trail of blood behind in his wake. His eyes dart from Adam to his front door and back again, but he doesn't turn around, afraid that if he does, he will falter and that will be it for him.

Adam's shrieks become muffled as a naked woman stuffs a fistful of crumpled paper money in his mouth, effectively gagging him. Grady frowns, thinking that the woman bears more than a resemblance to Adam himself. She could almost be the young man's sister. He decides that can't be possible. Instead, he must be going into shock—not thinking clearly, seeing things that aren't real. He takes two steps toward Adam, then stops again as the woman begins clawing up handfuls of grass and dirt, and shoves that into Adam's mouth, as well. Grady blinks his eyes but the woman still looks like she's related to her victim. Another naked man pinches Adam's nose shut. Adam squirms and wriggles, but is unable to break free.

Grady realizes that he can't outrun his pursuers. Even if he wasn't injured, they are younger and faster than he is, and their stamina seems to be fueled by their insanity. But neither does he have the courage to face them—to face his own demise and stare into their insane eyes. Keeping his own gaze fixed firmly on Adam, he watches as the younger man twitches and then lies still. Grady raises the pistol to his temple and hopes he has at least one bullet left in the gun. Then he closes his eyes.

"I'm sorry," he repeats, but this time, Grady is apologizing to himself.

Then, the car horn wails again. Grady opens his eyes in time to see Mendez smash through the attackers with his car, squashing both them and Adam underneath the grille. The young man's head bursts beneath one of the front tires. The other tire ruptures the stomach of the woman who looks like his sister. Broken ribs punch through her flesh, and she vomits blood, writhing in the car's wake. For a moment, Grady is reminded of a mortar attack he survived in Vietnam, and sees the faces of friends who died screaming, writhing in agony on the jungle floor as they bled out, mangled and torn.

The car's engine thrums, and Grady realizes that Mendez isn't slowing down. He screams as the vehicle veers toward him. Then, Mendez turns the wheel and it swerves away. His brake lights flash as he slides to a halt in front of Grady's apartment door, using the car as a partial blockade. He motions at Grady to run. Astonished, Grady does just that, moving as fast as age and his injury will allow. Out of the corner of his eye, Grady spots Phil and Beth careening toward the car, as well. He reaches the vehicle first, and clambers over the hood. The hot metal burns his hands, but Grady barely notices. He slides off the other side into the narrow space between his front door and the car's passenger door.

"I hope you have your keys," Mendez yells through the shattered passenger window.

Grady nods, because he's too winded to speak. He fumbles with the keys, pulling them from his pocket, but his hands are shaking too badly to select the correct one from the ring.

"Mr. Hicks," Phil shouts. "Mr. Mendez!"

"Hurry up," Grady yells. "Damn kids are gonna get themselves killed."

"Just get the door open," Mendez urges him, slipping out of the broken window. "They'll make it okay."

Grady slides the key into the lock and turns. The latch clicks and he throws the door open. Mendez nearly knocks him over rushing to get inside. Grady is about to rebuke him when Beth screams.

The horde has caught up to Phil and Beth, surrounding them, and cutting them off from Grady's front door. He takes aim with the pistol, but realizes that if he fires into the crowd, there's a good chance he'll hit one of the newlyweds instead.

"Drop down," he bellows. "I can't get a shot!"

"What are you doing?" Mendez yells. "Shut the door and get inside!"

"It's Phil and Beth. We've got to help them, goddamn it."

"We can't help them now. Don't be an idiot."

Before Grady can argue with him, he realizes that his neighbor is right. Phil swings the baseball bat savagely, trying to defend both his wife and himself, but he is quickly overwhelmed by the sheer number of foes. Someone hits him on the back of the head with a flashlight. Phil slows, and his shoulders slump. Another attacker lobs a broken cinder block, which cracks him in the ribs. Phil stumbles, reeling, and the crowd pulls him down. He desperately reaches for Beth, but she's wrenched away by more naked people. She slams her head backward, breaking one of their noses, and stomps on the arch of another's foot, freeing herself. Then, she tries to run toward the car, but the naked people shove her back into the fray. One man picks up Phil's baseball bat and swings, smashing Beth in the shoulder. Screaming, she doubles over, cradling her injured arm. A second blow knocks several teeth from her mouth, and her cries turn to gurgles. Someone else grabs a fistful of her hair and yanks her head up. The veins in her neck stand out like tree roots.

"No," Grady cries. "Oh God, no. Goddamn it…"

He raises the pistol again and fires a shot, hitting a nearby crazy in the chest. The wounded attacker topples backward, but five more are going to work on Beth with shovels and knives and chunks of masonry. One of her cheeks hangs down like a bloody mud-flap. Her eyes are wide. She's staring right at him.

Weeping, Grady realizes there is nothing he can do for the couple. He lowers the gun and closes the door behind him. When he closes his eyes, he can still see Beth's stare.

"Lock it," Mendez says.

Grady opens his eyes and wipes snot from his upper lip. "What good is that cheap little lock going to do against this shit?"

"It will buy us some time." Mendez speaks matter-of-factly, as if he were discussing how to program a DVD player, rather than referencing the army of killers marauding outside. "Even a few seconds can make a difference. And my car will slow them down, as well. They won't be able to get any leverage to beat your door down. We just need to barricade the windows. Hurry up."

"Phil and Beth are dead," Grady yelps. "So is Adam from across the way. Those people butchered them. Don't you care, Mendez? Don't you give a damn?"

Mendez shrugs. "People die every day, Grady. Tonight, it was them."

"That's some callous bullshit."

"Maybe so. I apologize if you are offended, but the fact remains—they're dead. I'm still alive. And I intend to stay that way."

He rushes into Grady's kitchen, and begins to push the refrigerator toward the windows. Shaking his head in dismay, Grady sets the gun down and goes to help him.

"Trust me," Mendez grunts as the heavy appliance scrapes across the floor, scratching the linoleum, "I can't die."

"What do you mean you can't die? Everyone can die. Nobody lives forever."

"I don't mean immortality," Mendez says. "I'm talking about here. Tonight. I can't die."

"Why the hell not?"

"As bad as things are right now? If I die, they're only going to get worse. Believe me."

"How so?"

"If I die tonight, then those people outside won't be the only things we have to worry about. There are things out there in the universe—things that want to exterminate us. I'm the only one that can keep us safe from them."

Grady decides that his neighbor has cracked under the strain. He doesn't exactly know Mendez well. The man travels a lot—always on the road. Grady thinks he's a salesman or something. But they greet each other in passing, and make small talk on occasion. Mendez has always seemed like a decent sort. Charming, smart, occasionally funny. He's never struck Grady as mentally ill—or what his daughter would call a whack-job.

Yes, Grady decides. *It must be stress. The poor man has snapped.*

"Let's just get this fridge moved," he says. "We can worry about dying later."

Eleven

Sam, Terri, Caleb, Stephanie, Mrs. Carlucci, Shaggy, and Turo: Apartment 1-D

Sitting on the floor in the corner of Sam's bedroom, Terri cradles Caleb in her lap, kissing the top of his head and rubbing his back and trying to reassure him. She hasn't held him like this in a while. He used to be cuddly when he was younger, but ever since he turned six, he's been less inclined. Sure, he still wants a kiss goodnight and he still hugs her on occasion and tells her that he loves her and that she is the Best Mommy Ever, but cuddle time has grown sparser. Terri dreads the day when it stops altogether. She wishes he would stay this age forever. She's terrified of him growing up. Terrified of him becoming a man.

But right now there are more immediate things to be terrified of.

She keeps her eyes on the hastily constructed barricade in front of Sam's bedroom door. All of the bookcases in the room have been stacked against it, as have his dresser, mattress, headboard, and box spring. Sam had a toolbox stored on the shelf in his closet and he, Stephanie, and Turo are currently nailing the headboard into the wall. Shaggy (Terri doesn't know if that's his nickname or his real name, and there hasn't been time to ask) stands guard, keeping his pistol at the ready. They can hear the group of crazy people on the other side of the door, beating at it and hammering on the walls, but so far, the blockade remains strong. Luckily, the chainsaw has stayed silent.

Mrs. Carlucci stands next to Terri and Caleb, peeking out the bedroom window. A few moments ago, the car motor fell silent. Now, that silence is filled by the sounds of breaking glass and pounding, and guttural growls and yelps.

Caleb stirs against her. "I want to go home, Mommy."

"I know, baby. I know."

"Not here. I mean home to Grandma's."

Terri wants to respond, but she can't. Her throat feels thick, and she begins to tremble, choking back the sobs welling up from deep inside of her.

Sam, Stephanie, and Turo stop hammering. All three are drenched in sweat. They step back and check their handiwork. Terri hears Sam murmur something about it holding. Shaggy mutters that it damn well better. Then he hands his gun to Turo and stretches, flexing and swiveling his arm, as if he has a cramp.

Mrs. Carlucci turns around and then slowly kneels. Terri can tell that the action pains the older woman. She grimaces, then smiles.

"Your name is Caleb, isn't it?"

Caleb nods. "Yes, Ma'am."

Mrs. Carlucci smiles again, but now Terri sees the fear behind her expression. "And very polite, I see. Well, Caleb, I'm Mrs. Carlucci. And you know what?"

"What?"

"I want to go home, too."

"Where do you live?" Caleb asks.

"Three doors down, with my little ones."

"Are you a grandma, too?"

Mrs. Carlucci laughs, and for a moment, the fear, pain, and unease are gone from her eyes.

"Bless your heart, no. No, I'm not a grandmother. But I have four kitties—Hannibal, King, Queenie, and Princess."

"How come Hannibal has a different name than the others?"

"Well, because I got him from a shelter. The people who had him before me named him that. I didn't think it would be right to change his name."

"Why did they take him to the shelter? Did they die? Maybe the Tick Tock Man got them, too."

Mrs. Carlucci frowns.

"The leader," Terri explains. "The…fat man."

"The ugly one who's head goes from side to side?" Mrs. Carlucci nods in understanding. "That's a good name for him. But no, Caleb, he didn't—"

"I agree it's a good name," Sam interrupts, "but it's about all we know right now. We need to figure this out."

"Maybe we should talk about it later," Turo says, his eyes and gun pointed at the barricade.

"I think it will hold," Sam replies. "I don't hear the chainsaw, and the hallway isn't wide enough for more than two of them, side-by-side. They might be able to get through, but it's going to take a while, and we'll hear them long before they do."

"I don't know about anybody else," Stephanie says, "but I could use a break."

"He's right," Shaggy agrees. "I could use one, too."

"She," Stephanie corrects him.

"What?"

"I'm a she, not a he."

"You're a he-she, more like it." Shaggy chuckles. "Ain't you still got a dick?"

"Hey!" Turo glances at him. "Dude, chill the fuck out with that shit."

"What? I'm just asking. Does he have a dick or don't he?"

"I don't know what Stephanie has," Sam says, stepping toward him. "But I've got this axe I stole from one of the fucks on the other side of the door. So why don't you lay off her?"

Shaggy puffs out his chest and flexes his arms again. "That supposed to be some kind of fucking threat? Look at you, all out of breath and wheezing. You gonna hit me with your pot belly? You gonna kill me in a fucking story?"

"Mommy," Caleb whispers. "Please, can't we leave here?"

"Excuse me," Terri interrupts, as Sam and Shaggy square off, "but my son is scared and so am I. Can we please figure out what we're going to do? What's happening?"

Everyone stares at her, not speaking. They glance at each other, and then back to her. Terri begins to feel very uncomfortable. Outside the bedroom, somebody pounds on the door.

"I want to go home," Caleb complains. "Right now!"

"I'm with him," Stephanie says. "What do we do?"

"We can't go out the window," Mrs. Carlucci informs them. "It's a twelve foot drop, and even if we don't break our legs, the backyard is full of them."

"Not if we land on the roof of the car," Turo says.

"The car is parked in front of the next apartment over. Only the trunk is under Sam's window."

"So, I'll land on the trunk."

Mrs. Carlucci shakes her head. "And then what? They'll surround you before you can get down."

Sam crosses the room, raises the axe, and points it at the wall. "We go through there."

Turo glances nervously at the barricade, as the sounds on the other side grow more insistent. "Say what?"

"Terri and Caleb's apartment is on the other side of this wall. And we all know how thin these walls are. We tunnel through, come out in their apartment, and hide inside until the coast is clear."

"I left my door open," Terri says. "What if they're inside my apartment, too?"

"I don't hear them over there," Sam says. "These... people... whatever you want to call them...they've been pretty noisy so far. Right now, they seem preoccupied with my apartment and the apartments downstairs. If we can get through this wall before they get through the door—and if we're careful—we can close Terri's front door without attracting attention."

"And then what?" Stephanie's tone is unconvinced. "As soon as they break in here, they'll see the hole in the wall and know where we went."

"What if we kept going?" Turo asks. "Go through all the walls, all the way down to the end of the building and shit. If they're still all here at this end, we might be able to sneak out, or at least get a head fucking start."

Shaggy shakes his head. "That's fucking crazy. We'd never make it."

"I don't think we have a choice," Sam says. "Like Mrs. Carlucci said, we can't go out the window."

"Maybe y'all can't," Shaggy says, "but Turo and I can. I've jumped farther than that before."

"Go ahead." Stephanie motions toward the window. "Good luck making it ten steps across the yard. Much as I'd love to see you go, though."

"Fuck you."

Stephanie winks. "No chance."

"Enough," Sam snaps, as the noise from the hallway grows louder. "If anybody's got any better ideas, now's the time."

Watching him take charge, Terri is reminded of her father. Most of the time, he'd been quiet and good-humored, but when the situation called for it, her father had been quite assertive, and able to command and lead others without question.

When nobody objects, Sam heaves the axe and tears into the wall. It sinks into the white plaster with a solid thunk, gouging several inches into the surface, but Terri is surprised by how little sound it makes.

"Got to admit," he says, "that I always wanted to try this."

Sam swings again. The axe blade cleaves through the wall, and plaster dust swirls around in the air.

"Wait," Stephanie says, picking up a claw hammer from the toolbox and pointing at the barricade. "Time your blows with theirs."

He nods. "Good idea. Just be careful you don't hit a power line."

"The electricity is out," Stephanie reminds him. "We shouldn't have to worry about it."

When the crazies beat on the door again, Sam and Terri simultaneously swing, digging further into the wall.

"It works." Sam sounds surprised. "Holy shit, we might actually do this!"

"Here, dude." Turo hands Shaggy the gun and grabs the other hammer from the toolbox. Then he joins them at the wall.

Terri feels guilty watching them work while she sits in the corner, but she also has Caleb to think about. She catches Mrs. Carlucci's eye.

"Could you sit with Caleb?"

"Of course, dear."

"Caleb, hop up, baby. Mommy wants to help the neighbors."

He stiffens, and for a moment, she's afraid that he'll resist. But when Mrs. Carlucci smiles at him, Caleb relaxes again, hopping off his mother's lap and plopping back down next to the older lady. Terri hears them discussing her cats as she walks over to the others.

"Do you have any more hammers?" Terri asks Sam.

"No, but you can use one of my award statues over there."

He points to a pile of books and other items that were hastily swept off the bookshelves. Among them are two haunted house statues with pointy-spired tips. They look like they're made of plastic, but when Terri picks one up, she realizes they are crafted from some sort of hard resin.

"They're pretty sturdy," Sam says. "You can smash

through the plaster with one of them. The little doors have a habit of falling off, but otherwise, they can take a beating. Believe me, I know. I got drunk once and threw one at..."

He trails off, suddenly seeming embarrassed. Instead of finishing, he turns his attention back to the wall, swinging far above Turo and Stephanie, who are gouging away near the floor, timing their blows with the ones barraging the bedroom door. Terri turns the award over in her hands. A small brass door flips open. Inside is a tiny engraved plaque that reads: *2001 SUPERIOR ACHIEVEMENT NONFICTION – THE DEVIL'S DUE – SAMUEL MILLER.*

Terri looks at him doubtfully. "Are you sure?"

"Absolutely," Sam grunts, hefting the axe for another blow. "I was going to sell them on eBay, but I didn't think I'd get much. Maybe if they help save our lives, they'll be worth more."

She crouches down next to Turo and Stephanie, and after a second of hesitation, slams the award statue against the wall. The spire snaps off, and a jolt runs up her arm. With her second blow, the plaster begins to give.

"That's it," Sam encourages the others. "Once we're through, we'll just hide out until the police arrive."

Terri notices that Turo stiffens for a moment when the police are mentioned. Then he goes back to work.

"They should have been here already," Mrs. Carlucci says. "I remember when they showed up right away. Not like now, where you call 911 and get put on hold."

"I think they're pretty busy," Stephanie says. "I called earlier and before we got cut off, the dispatcher said there were a lot of calls. I think...I think whatever is happening here happened there, as well."

"Where?" Sam asks.

"The emergency call center," Stephanie explains. "I think they broke in."

"At least you got through," Mrs. Carlucci replies. "The phones are down now. Maybe I should have gotten one of these mobile phones you young people use."

"They're not working either," Sam tells her. "I would imagine there's too many people trying to place calls. The network is jammed. Whatever is going on, it must be affecting a much bigger area than just here in the complex."

"But what is going on?" Terri chokes back a sob. She doesn't want to start crying in front of Caleb. He's already scared. Seeing his mother cry will just upset him even more. "No police, no phones, no electricity—"

"And a thousand naked crazy fuckers outside the door," Shaggy says. "Motherfuckers acting like they're on drugs or something."

Terri wants to ask him to watch his language in front of Caleb, but instead she holds her tongue.

"I'm sure we've all seen that in the news?" Sam asks. "The synthetic marijuana. What do they call that stuff— Spice? K2?"

"Black Mamba," Turo volunteers.

Sam shrugs. "I haven't heard that one, but whatever. People take those synthetic drugs, rip off their clothes, and go nuts."

"Usually in Florida," Stephanie quips. "But did you get a look at the people outside? They don't all look like drug users to me."

"True that," Turo agrees. "There were little kids."

"Old people, too." Stephanie glances at Mrs. Carlucci and Caleb. "No offense."

Mrs. Carlucci smiles. "None taken, sweetie."

"I even saw a cripple," Shaggy volunteers. "Naked bitch in a wheelchair."

"So what is it then?" Terri asks again. "What's causing this? Why are they like that?"

"Something in the water," Sam suggests. "Or maybe some kind of neurological attack? Maybe somebody released a gas or a chemical. If it was one of my books, I'd say it was caused by radiation from a comet, but this is real life."

"Maybe they're zombies," Shaggy says. "Like on The Walking Dead and shit."

"Fuck zombies," Sam mutters. "I said this is real life."

"Yeah?" Shaggy motions at the door with the gun. "Well, in real life, naked motherfuckers ain't trying to break down the doors and kill people. Maybe you need to reconsider what's real."

Terri sees Sam's jaw clench. He opens his mouth to reply, but then turns his attention back to the wall. He swings the axe again. This time, it cleaves through to the other side.

"That's it," Sam gasps. "We're through! Keep digging."

They renew their efforts, not bothering now to time their blows with the ones from the mob. Behind her, Terri hears Sam's bedroom door begin to splinter and crack.

"Hurry the fuck up," Shaggy warns. "They're almost through!"

Sam raises the axe and says, "Everybody out of the way."

Terri, Stephanie, and Turo move aside, and Sam attacks the wall, chopping and gouging, making the hole bigger. Terri watches as Turo goes over to Shaggy and whispers something. She can't hear what.

Shaggy says, "Man, the cops are the least of our fucking worries right now."

Before anyone else can respond to this, Stephanie holds up her hand. "Listen! Do you guys hear that?"

They all pause, listening. Out in the hallway, the pounding continues, but now someone is knocking below them, as well. They hear it directly beneath where they've been working, softly echoing up through the floor.

"Someone's alive down there," Terri says. "Knocking on the ceiling!"

"Not in our apartment," Shaggy says.

"No," Stephanie agrees. "It sounds like it's the next apartment over. Mr. Hicks?"

"Maybe we should dig through the floor," Terri suggests.

Sam shakes his head. "The floor's too thick. Lots of cement. And besides, how do we know it's not more of them?"

Stephanie nods. "Good point."

"I don't hear anything," Mrs. Carlucci admits.

"Turo," Sam says, "peek out the window and see what's going on out back. I want to make sure they're not trying to climb up here."

Sam turns his attention back to the wall. There is a loud crack behind the barricade. Terri tenses, expecting to see Tick-Tock barge through, but the furniture holds.

"They're clustered off to the side," Turo reports. "Around the car. Looks like they're trying to move it to get inside Mr. Hicks's apartment."

"So whoever is down there is one of us," Stephanie says. "One of our neighbors."

"We don't know that for sure" Sam says. "And even if it is Mr. Hicks, there's nothing we can do for him right now."

"That's cold," Turo says. "I mean, the old dude ain't very nice to Shaggy and me, but I don't want to see him get fucked up by these crazy assholes."

"I don't either," Sam agrees. "But what can we do to help him? Any ideas?"

Terri glances around the room. All of them are silent.

Stephanie sighs. "This sucks."

"Yeah." Sam nods "It does indeed suck. Okay, couple more swipes and this hole will be big enough. Get ready, just in case there are some of them in Terri's apartment."

Terri's heart hammers in her chest as she watches Sam swing the axe again. She makes her way across the room to Caleb, who leaves the comfort of Mrs. Carlucci's arms and flees to hers instead. Terri's tension eases somewhat as they embrace. She holds him close. Caleb hugs her back, squeezing tighter than he has in a long time.

"I love you," she whispers in his ear, "and I'm very proud of you. You know that, don't you?"

"I love you too, Mommy. It's going to be okay."

The makeshift barricade begins to shake as the mob focus their efforts on it. The crazies still aren't visible, but their voices fill the room. There are no words—just unintelligible growls and snarls.

Sam jumps back from the hole in the wall, axe at the ready. It's dark on the other side. Terri thinks of the boxes there in that darkness, filled with her and Caleb's lives. Then she thinks about Randy, and sees the fat man hacking through his head once again. She shudders. Caleb smooths her hair.

When no one comes charging through the hole trying to kill them, everyone in the room visibly relaxes.

"Okay." Sam turns to face them. "We're through. Let's grab one of these bookshelves. We'll pull it over the hole behind us. Shaggy, you've got the gun, so you go first."

"Fuck that. You got a gun, too. And you got an axe, motherfucker. Go ahead. I'm covering the door."

"Then you're in charge of moving the bookshelf." Sam turns to the wall and stares at a framed 11 x 15 picture of him and a dog. He sticks the frame in his waistband, and pulls his shirt down over it. Then he flexes and twists, as if testing to see if it will impede his movements. Apparently satisfied, he looks at the others. "Okay, everybody ready? Let's go."

He taps the axe head on the floor, knocking three times.

"What was that for?" Terri asks.

"I don't know," Sam admits. "To let whoever is down there know we're still alive, I guess? Or maybe to say I'm sorry."

Shrugging, he crouches down and, holding his weapon at the ready, creeps through the hole.

Twelve

The Exit and Grady:
Apartment 6-D

"I still don't think you should have done that," the Exit tells Grady as he binds gauze around the old man's injured ankle. "We don't know for sure who that is up there."

"I don't think it's these nudists," Grady replies. "It sounded like the neighbors."

"It sounded to me like somebody chopping through the wall. Why would the neighbors do that?"

Grady winces as the Exit finishes with his wound. The Exit takes no pleasure in this. He doesn't like to cause suffering in others, and only does it when he has to. Still, he is no stranger to blood or pain. He has been an agent of both and has inflicted both, in order to save the world. Tonight has been the first time he's ever had to inflict them to save himself. But then again, since the world will surely end if he dies, in saving himself, is he not saving the world?

The Exit is still unsure what is causing the evening's events. If it was a breach—if it was one of the others from outside the world—he's confident he would have known about it before this happened. He would have been able to stop it. There is always a warning before a breach occurs. He'd noticed none of the signs—no tingling in the back of his head, or static on the hairs of his arms, and the air hadn't felt like it did before a thunderstorm. He doesn't think the others are involved. This doesn't feel like their handiwork. There is nothing supernatural about what is occurring. So what, then? What would drive otherwise seemingly normal people to strip naked and run amok on a murderous rampage, indiscriminately slaughtering everyone in their path? A terrorist attack of some kind? Spiking the town's water supply with some form of hallucinogen? Doubtful. He remembers seeing signs of trouble long before he reached Red Lion. All of York County seemed to be effected. And since each town and borough had their own municipal water supply, it was unlikely someone could have simultaneously polluted them all. If the cause is indeed some sort of hallucinatory agent, then it's more likely it was airborne—some sort of gas or aerosol.

"They haven't knocked again," Grady whispers, staring up at the ceiling.

The Exit briefly follows his gaze. He hears pounding from another area above their heads, followed by a crash.

"It sounds to me like the mob is getting in upstairs."

Grady glances toward the barricaded door and windows. "Think we're okay down here?"

The Exit shrugs. "For now. The car is holding them back. They can't get around it to smash the door down. But we can't get out, either. And they know we're in here."

He places the gauze and medical tape on the kitchen table, next to a bottle of hydrogen peroxide and a tube of super glue, which he used to seal the gash in Grady's ankle.

"Thanks for fixing me up."

The Exit nods. "Of course. We'll need each other if we are going to survive this. I can't have you limping around, leaving a trail of blood behind us. Can you stand on it?"

"Only one way to find out."

Grady grips the side of the table and slowly rises from the chair. He tests his foot, putting a little weight on it, and then more. The Exit can tell by his posture that it hurts him to do so, but Grady's expression remains stoic.

"Good as new," he says, but his voice wavers.

"Okay. The first thing we should do is get away from these windows and move into one of the rear bedrooms.

We'll need to block up the windows back there, as well. I'm surprised they haven't broken in through those yet."

"Remember, those windows are at ground level, and they've got those bubbles over them."

The Exit frowns. "Bubbles?"

"Yeah, you know. Those plastic window well coverings?"

"Ah, yes."

"They've probably been so focused on the doors of the apartments above that they haven't even noticed the windows yet."

"That doesn't make sense."

"None of this makes sense, Mendez. But we can't go applying sense and logic to these people. Sensible folks don't run around naked while hacking and shooting people."

"Point. Do you have any other guns in the apartment?"

"No." Grady points at his pistol on the table. "Just that one. Got plenty of kitchen knives, though, and a bayonet I brought back from 'Nam."

The Exit stands and makes his way to the kitchen counter.

"First drawer on the right," Grady says.

The Exit pulls the drawer open and selects two knives—a broad-bladed butcher knife and a long, serrated bread knife. He examines them both and says, "These will do just fine."

"You want the bayonet, too?"

"No, you keep it. Judging by the numbers out there, sooner or later, you're going to run out of bullets. You should have a back-up weapon."

"If it comes to that, I'll use it on myself."

"That's a coward's way out."

Grady lunges toward him, catching him by surprise. Before the Exit can react, the old man clenches a fistful of his shirt. Grady exhales, stinking of denture cream and coffee. The Exit scowls.

"Coward? Don't talk to me about being a coward,

Mendez. I saw shit that makes what's going on outside look like a goddamn Disney cartoon."

"I'm not saying you didn't." The Exit keeps his tone calm and flat.

"Listen you weird fuck. I don't know what the hell you were on about earlier—all that you can't die bullshit, but if you want to stand here and call me a coward, then you're welcome to go wait outside with the other crazy bastards. If not, then back up off of me."

"I'm not doing anything, Grady. Indeed, you're the one holding my shirt."

Grady stares into his eyes, lips pulled back in a sneer. The Exit remains calm and unflinching. Sighing, Grady lets go.

"I'm sorry that I offended you," the Exit apologizes. "I didn't mean to imply that you're a coward. Obviously, you're not. You proved that just a few minutes ago. I just never saw suicide as a viable solution. But I'm also willing to admit that maybe it's just me. I personally won't choose that. I have too much to do. I'm too important."

Instead of responding, Grady shakes his head.

"Are we okay?" the Exit asks.

Grady shrugs.

"What are you thinking?"

Grady sighs again. "I'm thinking that these days, we don't really know most of our neighbors. And even when we think we do know them, we still don't. Not really."

"How so?"

"Well, take you for example. All this time, I thought you were just some traveling businessman. Nice enough guy. Quiet. Kept to yourself mostly. I had no idea until tonight that you suffer from delusions of fucking grandeur."

"I'm not crazy." This time, the Exit can't keep the edge from his voice.

"Then get a little crazy," Grady whispers. "Because you might need it to survive tonight. Trust me on that. I've been there. You think you're so important that you've got to live? Then get in touch with your crazy side. I…"

He trails off, closing his eyes. When he opens them again, the Exit sees tears forming.

"You're thinking about Phil and Beth and that other neighbor?" the Exit asks.

"Adam." Grady nods. "But not just them, though."

"What's wrong?"

"I…I shot that kid out there, Mendez. I killed that boy."

"A boy who was trying to kill you, Grady."

"I know…" Grady chokes back sobs. "But still…shit…"

The Exit frowns, wondering what to do. He knows that he should offer his neighbor some sort of comfort, but he's not sure how. It has been a long time since he's had a conversation like this—since he's interacted with another human being in any matter other than closing doorways. His dealings with other people are mostly trivial—thanking a waitress for bringing more coffee, telling a store clerk he'll be paying cash, giving directions to a lost motorist at a highway rest area. The only lengthy conversations he has are with his sacrifices, and those discussions are always the same—the sacrifices plead for their lives, and he tries to gently reassure them that their death is important, and noble, and unavoidable. For too long he has granted comfort and consolation by sliding a blade across the throats of the grieving. He has trouble remembering what other ways are considered acceptable in society.

"It's going to be okay," the Exit says, because it seems like an acceptable thing to say, even if he doesn't believe it.

"No, it's not. I've seen some shit in my life, but this…"

"I agree, things are bad. But let's stay focused. You were in the army, right?"

Grady nods sadly.

"Then you know it is best to stay occupied. You need to keep your mind from wandering. Let's get the bedroom secured so you're not dwelling on what happened outside."

Grady wipes his nose with his shirt sleeve. "Okay. You're right."

He retrieves the pistol from the kitchen table and limps out of the kitchen. The Exit follows him. They're halfway down the hall when a loud bang startles them both. It's the sound of metal on metal. Both men spin around, and then stare at each other.

"What the hell?" Grady whispers.

The Exit motions at him to stay there. Then he returns to the living room and peeks out of the barricaded window. A cluster of naked people have gathered around the car. One of them has a sledgehammer. As the Exit watches, he swings it over his head and brings it smashing down on the car once again. His compatriots cheer, fists raised triumphantly, and waving their weapons over their heads. All four of the car's tires have been slashed, and the windshield and windows are completely shattered now. The Exit backs away from the window.

"Mendez," Grady calls. "What is it?"

The Exit hurries down the hall and grabs the old man by the arm. "Come on. We've got to get to work. We are running out of time."

Grady closes the bedroom door behind them, and fumbles around in the dark. The Exit pauses, letting his eyes adjust to the gloom. The chaos is louder on this side of the apartment. The light dangling from the ceiling shakes back and forth as feet pound above them. They hear wood breaking and the sound of hammering. The walls seem to reverberate from the blows.

"They're in Sam's apartment," Grady says.

"Yes, which is why I don't think you should have tapped on the ceiling. What are you doing?"

"Reloading," Grady says. "And pocketing the extra bullets. Hang on a minute."

The Exit hears him shuffling around some more. Drawers open and close.

"Keep the noise down," he warns. "We don't want them to hear us."

"I'm trying to find some matches," Grady explains. "I've got a candle on the nightstand. Some scented thing I've never used. My daughter got it for me."

"Don't," the Exit warns. "Granted, this is a basement level apartment, but they might still be able to see the glow from the parking lot."

"Not through these curtains, they won't. Believe me, I know. I peep through them all the time, with nobody the wiser."

The Exit suspects that the old man is doing exactly what he suggested—keeping busy in an effort to avoid thinking about the kid he shot. Still, lighting a candle seems like a foolish thing to do.

"Later," he says, trying to stay patient. "First, help me barricade this door. And let's do it quietly."

They strip the mattress and box spring off Grady's bed and stand them up against the door. Then they try to lift the dresser, but it's too heavy and unwieldy, and the Exit finds that he's doing most of the work. Instead, they inch it across the floor. The carpet muffles most of the sound, for which the Exit is grateful.

Groaning, Grady crouches down in the dark and slumps against the wall.

"Now what?" he asks.

"Now," the Exit replies, "we wait, and try to come up with a better plan before they get inside."

"It doesn't bother you, does it?"

"What?"

"All those people you ran over with your car."

"No," the Exit admits. "It doesn't bother me."

"I'm not judging you," Grady explains. "I knew guys like that in Vietnam, too. They just shut down. Block it out. To be honest, I was always a little envious of that."

The Exit shrugs. "We do what we have to do to stay alive. Like I said before, I'm not dying here tonight. I can't."

Then he starts thinking about a way to make sure that happens.

Thirteen

Sam, Terri, Caleb, Stephanie, Mrs. Carlucci, Shaggy, and Turo: Apartment 2-D

Clutching her butcher knife and the hammer, Stephanie stands with the others, waiting quietly in the darkness of Terri and Caleb's unoccupied bedroom, while Sam sneaks forward and closes the apartment's front door. She grips the tools tightly, holding her breath until her pulse pounds in her throat, positive that at any minute, they'll be discovered and their attackers will charge in after them.

Instead, Sam creeps back into the bedroom. He's got the axe in one hand and his pistol tucked in his waistband. His expression is one of shocked relief.

"They see you?" Shaggy asks.

"No." Sam shakes his head. "They're so preoccupied with my apartment that they didn't even notice."

"Tick Tock?" Stephanie asks.

"No, I didn't see him. And I wasn't inclined to look further."

"So," Terri asks, "are we safe here?"

"Safe?" Sam laughs—a dry sound, more like a cough. "Hell no. I locked the door, but that's all. If I started moving furniture to block it, they'd have heard me. And sooner or later, they're going to get into my bedroom. Then they'll know where we went."

"So," Stephanie asks, "what do we do now?"

"Stick with our plan," Sam says. "I think it's solid. When I shut the door, I noticed that the parking lot in front of Mrs. Carlucci's apartment is empty. They're all clustered on this side of the building, and—I guess—out back in the yard. If we can make it through the walls to Mrs. Carlucci's, and the coast is still clear, then we can run into the woods."

"That's a lot of ifs," Turo replies. "I'm starting to think Shaggy is right. Maybe we should jump out the fucking window into the backyard."

Sam sighs. Stephanie can tell he's annoyed and exasperated.

"If you guys want to do that," he says, "then I won't stop you. But can you at least wait until we've tunneled through the next wall?"

"How come?"

"Because the moment you jump out of the window, they're going to see which apartment you came from. Give us a head start, for God's sake."

Turo nods. "Alright. That's fair enough."

"Yo," Shaggy says. "If they start mobbing up in here, I'm out the fucking window, head start or no. Just so we're all clear on that."

"Chivalry is not dead," Stephanie quips. "Come on. Let's get started."

She heads toward the bedroom door. A pyramid of boxes are stacked against one wall. All of them are marked as belonging to Caleb. She realizes this would have been the little boy's room. She wonders what this must be like for him—to have gone through all the excitement and uncertainty of moving to a new place, and then having that shattered by a murderous mob of crazies led by a fat man with some sort of nervous twitch. The only other items in the room are some clothes hangers in the closet and an air conditioner in the window. It's the same one Stephanie has in her apartment, provided by the Pine Village management. She wonders if they got a discount for buying the units in bulk.

Pausing, Stephanie looks back at Shaggy. "You pulled the bookshelf over the hole in the wall?"

"Yeah. Why?"

Ignoring him, she turns her attention to Sam. "Maybe we should stack some of these boxes over the hole on this side? Help slow them down?"

"Good idea," Sam agrees. "Turo and Shaggy, can you guys do that while we get started on the wall?"

Both men grumble about it, but nod, conceding.

"I'll help," Terri volunteers. "Caleb, you go with Mrs. Carlucci."

"But I want to stay here," he insists. "They're my toys, Mom."

"Do what I asked. It's safer for you to go with them. Go on now."

"Come on, Caleb." Mrs. Carlucci takes the boy's hand. "You can watch me dig through the wall."

"Are you sure you're up for it?" Stephanie asks.

"My cats are alone, and we've got two more walls to go through before I can get to them. Stand back and watch me. I'll out-dig all of you. I've got no time for nonsense."

She winks, and Stephanie can't help but smile at the old woman's spirit—and her concern for her cats.

Caleb takes the elderly neighbor's hand. "Do you think your cats are okay?"

"King, Queenie, and Princess have been pampered their whole lives. They're sort of...soft. But Hannibal will take care of them. He's a wily one."

"Like the coyote?"

It takes Stephanie a second to understand the reference, but Mrs. Carlucci picks up on it right away. Chuckling, she leads Caleb out of the room. Stephanie turns and spots Terri, box in hand, watching her son go. There are tears in the young mother's eyes.

Then there are tears in Stephanie's eyes, as well.

"It's going to be okay," Sam tells them as they enter the other bedroom.

Stephanie nods, afraid that if she tries to speak, she might break down and wail instead. Her chest aches, and each heartbeat feels like a hammer blow. She thinks about her parents, and hopes they are okay.

Terri's bedroom is much like Caleb's, except that there are more boxes. A disassembled bed has been stacked against the wall, but there is no mattress or box spring. Stephanie assumes they must still be outside in the truck. The window holds another identical air conditioner.

"Stand back," Sam says, approaching the far wall. "I'll get us started."

Mrs. Carlucci guides Caleb over to the window. Stephanie follows them. As she does, she realizes that the room isn't as dark as it was a moment before. She glances at the window and sees a flickering light reflected in the glass. She leans her forehead against the window and peers outside. The smooth surface is cool against her skin, but there's no time to enjoy the sensation. A naked woman is running across the yard with a red metal gasoline can. Crazies on both sides of her clear a path and cheer wildly. Stephanie's eyes go wide as she sees another nude man trotting along behind the woman. He holds a blazing torch high over his head.

"Um, Sam?"

A solid thunk echoes as the axe blade strikes the wall.

"What, Steph?"

THUNK

"You might want to see this."

He turns to look at her, axe half-raised for another blow. Then, shoulders sagging, he crosses the room.

"Better hurry," Stephanie urges.

Sam stands next to her and peers out the window. "Oh, shit…"

"They're going to light the car on fire," Mrs. Carlucci says.

Sam nods. "And the complex will follow. Everybody stand back."

He yanks back the curtains and raises the axe. Stephanie is about to ask what he's doing, concerned that the mob in the backyard will spot the movement. Then Sam begins running the axe blade along the rubber molding between the air conditioner and the windowsill, slicing through it. The unit trembles as he does so. Stephanie notices the framed photograph Sam tucked into his waistband earlier. It looks like it is about to fall out. She's about to mention it when he grunts with exertion. He slams the axe against each side of the air conditioner, smashing the plastic supports that bolt the unit to the wall. The air conditioner tilts forward, gouging the windowsill. The frame shakes.

"Give me a hand," he grunts, glancing back at Stephanie.

She sets her knife and hammer aside, and glances out the window as she rushes to Sam's side. Outside, the woman with the gas can has clambered up onto the roof of the car. As the other attackers cheer, she begins to unscrew the lid. The runner with the torch has almost reached the vehicle, as well.

"Push!" Stephanie digs her feet into the carpet.

The air conditioner groans, its metal casing squealing against the windowsill as she and Sam shove it free. Too late, Stephanie realizes that the unit is still plugged in. The black power cord snaps tight against the wall, and the air conditioner dangles for a second. Then, the cord rips free from the electrical socket and the air conditioner plummets below, followed by a sickening thud. The sound reminds Stephanie of after Halloween, when her parents would allow her to drop the starting-to-rot pumpkins off the porch roof.

She leans out the open window and peers below. The woman's head looks much like those splattered pumpkins used to. It's smashed flat, and spread out. Brains and blood and skull fragments are scattered like pumpkin seeds and pulp.

"Out of the way," Sam barks, pushing forward.

He aims his pistol out the open window and fires two rounds at the torch runner. Both shots miss. The mob roars in anger. Gritting his teeth, Sam fires three more rounds. Over Sam's shoulder, Stephanie sees the torch bearer fall. The flaming brand tumbles from his hand, setting the grass on fire. The naked people crane their necks upward, gnashing their teeth and glaring.

"They know we're here now," Stephanie mutters.

"Yes," Sam shouts, running back to the wall, "they damn sure do. Let's dig!"

Startled, Stephanie stifles a scream as Terri, Shaggy, and Turo run into the room, glancing around wildly.

"The fuck is happening?" Shaggy demands.

"They tried to set the building on fire," Stephanie says.

"Those crazy motherfuckers in Sam's apartment heard the shots," Turo shouts. "They're coming through, and them boxes ain't gonna hold them."

Sam attacks the wall, swinging with wild abandon. Stephanie starts to help him when she hears the boxes come crashing down in the other bedroom. Simultaneously, somebody begins pounding relentlessly on Terri's front door.

"They're in!" Stephanie rushes across the bedroom and slams the door. "Help me block it!"

Except for Sam, the others stand frozen with panic. Stephanie isn't even sure they heard her.

"I'm through," Sam yells, standing back from the hole. "Everyone hurry!"

This seems to snap them out of their stupor. They begin running for the wall.

Stephanie locks the door and stands with her back to it, hyperventilating. The walls shake as, out in the living room, the front door is smashed down. The apartment echoes with the sounds of pounding feet and wild, inarticulate cries. Seconds later, someone slams into the bedroom door. Shrieking, Stephanie runs away from it. The knob is jiggled violently, and the door rattles in its frame.

Orange light flickers from the open window as the fire in the yard slowly spreads. Stephanie smells smoke, and hears people roaring outside.

Sam ducks down and clambers through the hole in the wall. Mrs. Carlucci, Terri, and Caleb follow. All of them are screaming. Wide-eyed, Stephanie glances at Shaggy and Turo as more blows rain down upon the door.

"Go," Turo says, nodding at the hole. "We got this shit! We'll be right behind you."

"But—"

Shaggy levels his gun at the door. "Hurry the fuck up, bitch!"

Stephanie hates herself for it, but in that moment, she finds herself hoping Shaggy will get killed in the next few seconds.

"It's okay," Turo assures her, perhaps noticing her hesitation. "Just go."

Stephanie ducks her head low and crawls through the hole, emerging in her own spare bedroom. Then she turns to look into the other apartment. Sam rushes to her side and beckons at Shaggy and Turo.

"Come on, guys!"

"We're good," Turo insists. "Just—"

Terri's bedroom door bursts open, slamming against the wall. The force and suddenness causes Shaggy to stagger backward toward the window. Tick Tock stands in the doorway, his bulk filling the space. He leers at them, drool running down his chin. There are bloody handprints smeared across his glistening, fish-belly white flesh. Stephanie spots an icepick in his left hand. The weapon seems very small in his massive fist. The handle is concealed beneath his sausage-like fingers.

Shouting, Turo lunges forward and swings his claw hammer at the giant. Still grinning, Tick Tock catches Turo's wrist and yanks him closer. Before anyone can move, his left hand flicks forward with a speed that belies his size. He rapidly stabs Turo in both eyes. Blood and something that looks like watered down petroleum jelly dribbles down Turo's cheeks. Then, Tick Tock pulls him out into the hall. Turo shrieks in agony as three more crazies charge through the door. Shaggy shoots two of them while screaming his friend's name.

Something explodes next to Stephanie's ear, startling her so badly that she drops her weapons. She realizes that it's Sam, who is also firing into the onrushing horde. Four more naked people rush through the door, but their entrance is impeded by the bodies of their fallen comrades, allowing Shaggy and Sam to pick them off. Stephanie's ears begin to ring. The gunshots are so loud that her teeth hurt. Sam shouts something at Shaggy, but she can't hear what it is, even though he's right next to her.

Shaggy raises his weapon and stalks toward the open door, stepping over the bodies. Stephanie sees him mouthing Turo's name, and realizes that he's yelling, but she's still deafened by the blasts. There is a flash of movement from out in the hallway, and she catches a brief glimpse of Tick Tock's Hello Kitty tattoo. Then, something like a misshapen soccer ball is flung into the room. It lands near Shaggy's feet and rolls twice. It takes Stephanie a second to realize that the object is Turo's severed head, which is still bleeding from the eyes and the frayed stump of a neck. The handle of the icepick juts from one of his ears.

It is followed a moment later by Turo's penis and one of his hands. Gristle hangs from each, glistening in the dark. Stephanie's eyes lock on the severed penis. It looks like some sort of small, hairless rodent lying there on the floor. Her nails dig into the carpet, as she fights the urge to vomit.

Turo's other hand is flung into the room. After that comes something long and slick. At first she thinks it's a sausage. Then she realizes it's a part of Turo's intestines.

Stephanie is aware of Sam clutching her arm, trying to pull her away from the hole, but she doesn't move. She feels rooted to the spot. Her eyes dart from the dismembered body parts to the door and then to Shaggy. All of the fight seems to have gone out of him. He simply stares at his friend's head in horror, his arm hanging limp at his side, gun pointed at the floor.

Stephanie's ears are still ringing, but her hearing starts to return because the cries from out in the hall grow louder. Then she realizes it's not cries, but taunts. The mob is jeering them.

Tick Tock points at Shaggy and laughs. Glowering, Shaggy raises his pistol. Before he can fire a shot, the behemoth moves aside and the horde pours into the room.

Shaggy shouts, "This ain't over you fat fuck!"

He turns and dives out the open window, disappearing so quickly that it's almost like he was never there.

Then, Stephanie and Sam scramble backward as the howling crowd rushes toward them.

Fourteen

Shaggy:
The Yard

Shaggy belly-flops onto the roof of the car, knocking the air from his lungs. The pain is the worst thing he's ever felt in his life. Stunned, he can only lay there for a moment, mouth hanging open, drooling all over the hot metal. He tries to breathe and finds that he can't. Moving is just as difficult. Even seeing clearly is a struggle. In addition to the pain in his ribs, his back feels like it is on fire. He remembers scraping it against the windowsill as he jumped. He wonders how bad the wound is.

Finally, he draws breath—an exercise in agony. Shaggy moans, writhing. The car's suspension squeaks and groans.

He closes his eyes and sees Turo's penis landing on the floor in front of him again. It is only then that Shaggy realizes he is crying.

He opens his eyes again and finds enough breath to scream. The mob answers in kind. Panicked, Shaggy realizes that he's dropped the Kimber. Struggling for air, he pushes himself up on his arms and knees, and glances around for it. He spies the .45 lying on the hood of the engine. He scrambles across the roof, fingernails screeching on the paint, and leans out over the windshield, desperately grasping for the weapon.

A naked man crawls onto the hood. His body shows the tell-tale signs of extended chemotherapy, and Shaggy wonders how he has the strength to move, let alone attack him. The man swings a brick, intent on smashing Shaggy in the head, but he grabs the attacker's wrist with his left hand, stopping the blow. Shaggy can't help but think of Turo and Tick Tock, who were just in a similar position only moments

124

ago. The man's skin feels like tissue paper. Shaggy squeezes, grinning as his fingers grind against bone. Then, his other hand closes around the handle of the gun. Still clutching the chemo patient's frail wrist, he raises the Kimber, shoves it under the man's chin, and squeezes the trigger. The top of the attacker's head explodes like a volcano, showering Shaggy and the rest of the crowd at the front of the car in gore. Shaggy releases the man's wrist and lets his limp form topple backward onto the hood. The man's head is still spewing blood as he falls.

Shaggy licks his lips, tasting salt. He frowns, wondering why his face is so wet. Then he realizes just what it is he's tasting, and shudders in revulsion.

"Oh, fuck..."

Blinking blood from his eyes, Shaggy staggers to his feet. He's still having trouble catching his breath, and he's aware of a sharp pain in his left side. He picks off four more attackers, and moves backward toward the edge of the car's roof, with the apartment complex at his back. He wants to risk a glance upward, to see if any of his neighbors are going to help him, but he's afraid to take his eyes off the mob surrounding him. He wonders idly if Turo could still be alive up there, maybe looking down at him right now. Then he remembers once again what happened, and realizes that would be hard for Turo to do without a head—or his other parts, for that matter.

Realizing that he's in shock, Shaggy shakes his head and plants his feet, looking around for a way to escape. He takes another step backward, and almost slips in a pile of gore. That's when he notices the dead woman on the roof with him. Her head is nothing but a bloody smear and ragged flaps of skin, dripping down onto the shattered rear window. An air conditioner juts from the wreckage, surrounded by sparkling chunks of glass. Next to it is an unopened gas can.

Shaggy prods the corpse with his foot, and sends it tumbling down to the ground. He looks out at the enraged crowd. About two dozen naked figures surround the car. Many of them are armed, but he doesn't see any guns among them. At the fringe of the mob, flames dance. Shaggy realizes that the yard is on fire. So are several crazies, running about wildly, shrieking and flapping their arms and managing to spread the flames further. Thick plumes of smoke curl up into the air, obscuring anything beyond them. As he watches, the wind shifts, and the haze drifts toward the car.

"What's wrong, motherfuckers? You want some of this? Bring it!"

Shaggy doesn't necessarily want them to bring it, but challenging them makes him feel braver, so he does it again.

"What you got? You ain't got nothing! You don't want none of this! Fuck you."

Then, the crowd surges forward, proving him wrong. Naked figures climb up onto the trunk and the hood, reaching for him, while others gather around the driver's side, stabbing and swinging at him with various ranged weapons—shovels, rakes, makeshift spears fashioned from broken broom handles, a garden hoe, a hockey stick, and even a simple tree branch.

"Shit..."

Shaggy fires three shots toward the trunk, two at the attackers in front of him, and one to his right, at the people on the hood. When the gun clicks empty, he panics.

"Shit, shit, shit, shit."

Dodging a vicious blow from a shovel, he fumbles in his pants pocket for his spare magazine. The wielder of the shovel, a man Shaggy recognizes as the owner of the tricked out black Nissan in Building B, swings the weapon again. Shaggy pulls his hand from his pocket, grabs the shovel, and wrenches it from the man's hands. He quickly jams the pistol in his waistband. Then he swings his new weapon, slamming the flat end of the shovel upside a woman's head as she crawls onto the roof. Even over the noise from the crowd, Shaggy can hear the wet snap her jaw makes as it breaks. The woman falls back onto the hood, knocking over the other attackers behind her. They wriggle beneath her body, struggling to free themselves from the tangle.

Shaggy lashes out once more with the shovel, burying the blade in the Nissan owner's face. It slashes through the man's cheek, carving the flesh from his mouth to his ear, and broadening his smile. Shaggy catches a glimpse of broken teeth and pulped gums. The man's mouth is filled with blood. Despite his obvious distress, the man continues to grin. Shaggy returns the gesture. Then he shoves hard on the handle. The man stumbles backward, taking the embedded shovel with him.

He paws at his pocket again, trying to free the spare magazine. This time, he succeeds. Shaggy ejects the spent clip, letting it clatter onto the car roof, and slams the new one in place. Then he opens fire again, picking targets from left to right and then back again. Bodies begin to pile up around the car. The fire in the yard creeps closer to him. When he breathes in—an act that causes the sharp pain in his side to get worse—he tastes smoke in the back of his throat.

He hears a muffled crash from inside the apartment behind him, but doesn't dare turn around. Instead, he stay's focused on the mob, head swiveling back and forth, picking them off as they try to rush him. Shaggy drops seven more targets before it occurs to him to wonder how many shots he has left. There can't be many. He debates saving one for himself, and then decides against it. He still owes Tick Tock for Turo. Shaggy has never had many people in his life he could count on. Girlfriends seem to stick around only as long as his money or his drugs hold out. The same goes for friends.

He hasn't spoken to his parents since they kicked him out of the house when he was still a senior in high school. The same goes for his older brother—the college boy and apple of his parents' eyes, always talking about white privilege and third wave feminism and how everything is fucking problematic. He's an academic douchebag. Shaggy wonders briefly where they are now. His brother is a professor at nearby York College, and his parents still live in Spring Grove, only thirty minutes away by car, on the other side of the county. Is what's happening here happening there, as well?

If so, then good. Fuck them.

Turo was one of the few friends who had stood by him. He'd never fronted. Never tried to get over on him. He was always willing to share, be it drugs or booze or pussy—or even money when he had it (which wasn't often). Turo always had Shaggy's back, and now he was lying on the floor upstairs, dissected by some sick naked fucks. They'd cut his head off, and his hand. Hell, they'd cut off his fucking dick! So no. Fuck no. No he wasn't going to save a bullet for himself. He was going to save it for that Pillsbury Doughboy-looking motherfucker with the Hello Kitty tattoo.

"Fuck this. Not yet, you motherfuckers. Not fucking yet."

Shaggy drops down into the narrow space between the car and the apartment building. The soles of his feet vibrate as he hits the cement, and he grunts as a fresh burst of pain tears through his side. It feels like he's got a knife in there, twisting in his guts. The pain gets worse when he breathes again.

He fires two more shots over the roof, targeting the first two naked people to climb up onto the car. The crazies beat against the vehicle with their fists and weapons, and then they smash out the driver's side windows and unlock the doors. He puts his fist against the passenger window and extends his middle finger. Then he raises the .45 for another shot.

Before he can squeeze the trigger, the apartment door opens behind him.

"Get in here, you damn fool!"

Shaggy glances over his shoulder and sees an elderly black man standing in the doorway. He recognizes the guy as his neighbor, but realizes that he doesn't know the old man's name.

"Come on, dumbass. Don't make me say it again."

Without responding, Shaggy lunges through the open doorway, wincing in pain. Wisps of smoke dog his heels, as the fire in the yard grows larger. Inside the apartment is another man—middle aged, Hispanic. Shaggy can't be sure, but he thinks the guy lives in the apartment next to this one, two doors down from him and Turo. The man nods at him, seemingly calm and placid.

The old man slams the door and locks it. Then he turns to Shaggy.

Shaggy tries to speak, but can only gasp for air. He nods instead.

"Well," the old man barks. "Don't just stand there. Help us get this barricade back in place."

Fifteen

Sam, Terri, Caleb, Stephanie, and Mrs. Carlucci : Apartment 3-D

"Stephanie," Mrs. Carlucci shouts as she runs through the girl's apartment, "where's your hair spray?"

"What? I can't hear…"

"Your hair spray! There's no time for nonsense now. Where is it?"

"In my bedroom. On my dresser."

"And a cigarette lighter? Matches? Anything like that?"

"Um…"

"Think!"

"I've got an incense burner on my dresser. Check that. There should be a lighter next to it."

The young woman sounds flustered. Mrs. Carlucci can't say that she blames her, given that a horde of howling, naked madmen (and women…and children) are scrabbling at the hole in the wall, trying to pursue them. The only reason they haven't so far is because Sam and Stephanie are crouched in front of the wall, holding them back. At this range, Sam is having no trouble shooting them. Sam's revolver holds five shots. Every time he's empty, Stephanie puts her butcher knife and claw hammer to work, hacking, slashing, and beating anyone who tries to crawl through the hole, while he hurriedly reloads. Both the knife and the hammer are slick with blood. The walls and the floor are spattered with it, as well. It drips from the broken plaster, pooling with the dust and debris.

After climbing through the hole, Terri and Caleb fled for the living room. Now, as Mrs. Carlucci makes her way through the dark, the two of them nearly run her over.

Although it's hard to see in the gloom, she can tell that their eyes are wide with panic.

"They're trying to break down the door," Terri pants, breathless.

"Take the axe," Sam calls, firing through the hole again. The flash from the barrel illuminates both him and Stephanie. Mrs. Carlucci sees the terror etched on their faces, as deeply as the lines and creases on her own. Those lines were created by time. She wonders what new lines she'll have tomorrow, born out of fear.

Then she wonders if she'll even be alive tomorrow to find out.

"Grab the axe," she yells so that Terri can hear her over the gunshots.

The young mother does as she's told. Mrs. Carlucci grabs both Terri and Caleb by the hands and hurries them toward Stephanie's bedroom. They hear the front door shuddering in its frame as they dash down the hall. Mrs. Carlucci frowns, knowing that the door won't hold much longer, and that sooner, rather than later, Sam and Stephanie will be overrun.

"Start digging through the wall," she orders as they enter the bedroom. "My apartment is on the other side. Caleb, I know you're scared, but make sure you stay out of your mommy's way."

"Why bother?" Terri asks. "Maybe we should just go out the window like Shaggy did."

"Shaggy was a drug-addled idiot," Mrs. Carlucci snaps, rummaging through Stephanie's vanity table. "I've got little patience for his sort of nonsense, or that of his friend, may he rest in peace."

"But…"

"Do you really want your little boy to jump twelve feet into that crowd below unless we absolutely have no choice? Get through the wall. I've got more bullets for my gun on the other side, and my cats are over there, alone and probably as terrified as we are. Now, quit wasting time and start digging!"

"Okay."

Without another word, Terri goes over to the wall and begins to chip away. She's tentative with the first few blows, but then she takes to it with fervor. Plaster dust swirls through the shadows. Satisfied that the girl is now focused on their survival rather than panicking, Mrs. Carlucci turns her attention back to the vanity. It's a beautiful piece of furniture, fashioned from dark hickory and equipped with an ornate mirror. A hair dryer and a curling iron dangle off the side of the mirror, supported by their power cords. The top of the vanity is full of perfumes, hair products, beauty creams, make-up, cotton balls, and assorted jewelry. Mrs. Carlucci nods with approval, impressed by the brand names she sees. For a young woman who used to be a young man, Stephanie certainly knows what to buy, and what not to waste her money on. If she continues to do so, she should have beautiful skin for a long time to come.

Provided they make it through this, of course.

She grabs two aerosol cans of hairspray from the tabletop, along with another of spray-on deodorant. Then she hurries over to Stephanie's dresser. It takes her a moment to spot the incense burner in the darkness. It's a small, ceramic cone sitting in the middle of a glass ashtray. A packet of incense sticks are on the dresser next to it, along with a red plastic cigarette lighter. She retrieves the lighter, accidentally knocking the incense packet to the floor. Then, with two of the aerosol cans tucked under her arm and the other in hand, she hurries back to the other room. The battering on the living room door is even louder as she rushes past it this time.

"Get back," she yells.

Stephanie glances her way, but Sam is oblivious. He

fires another shot at point blank range, killing an attacker on the other side. That room—the empty bedroom in Terri and Caleb's apartment—is now littered with naked corpses, most of whom have been shot to death, but a few of which have been slashed by Stephanie. As a result, the crazy people are having trouble overrunning them, because the hole is choked with the dead.

"Sam!" Mrs. Carlucci drops the cans and taps him on the shoulder. "Get out of the way! Guard the front door. Stephanie, you go help Terri get through that last wall."

Sam frowns. "Mrs. Carlucci…what are you—?"

"STAND BACK, DAMN IT!"

Visibly shocked, Sam and Stephanie comply, scurrying out of her way. Two more naked people charge the hole in the wall. As they start to crawl over the bodies surrounding the opening, Mrs. Carlucci raises the can of hair spray, presses the button, and flicks the cigarette lighter in front of the stream. The effect is instantaneous. A bright gout of flame bursts forth, as she transforms the hair spray into a homemade flamethrower. She sprays it back and forth in an arc, torching both attackers and setting their heads ablaze. They recoil, shrieking in agony. Behind her, Sam and Stephanie whoop and cheer in triumph and disbelief. Mrs. Carlucci extinguishes the cigarette lighter. Rather than turning to face her neighbors, she keeps her attention on the other room.

"You're like MacGyver," Sam says.

"I don't know who that is," Mrs. Carlucci responds.

"Neither do I," Stephanie admits. "Who's MacGyver?"

"It's a TV show! Richard Dean Anderson?"

Mrs. Carlucci glances at them in time to see Stephanie frown.

"You mean the guy from Stargate?" Stephanie asks.

"Sam," Mrs. Carlucci interrupts. "Guard the door. If they

133

get through, start shooting. Stephanie, go help Terri. I've got this covered."

"I guess you do," Sam replies.

The two of them hurry off. Mrs. Carlucci turns her attention back to the hole in the wall. Suddenly she feels very small and alone. Then, another attacker rushes forward, and there's no time to think anymore. She unleashes another stream of fire, and the attacker recoils.

From the other room, she hears Terri cry out with effort, hears the thud of the axe hitting the wall. Mrs. Carlucci wonders what her cats must think of all this noise. They're probably frightened to death, the poor things—even Hannibal. Her eyes well up, thinking about their probable distress. When another naked person tries to crawl through the hole, Mrs. Carlucci snarls. She blasts them right in the face. Screaming, the attacker scurries backward and begins rolling around on the floor, trying to extinguish the flames.

The air stinks—a miasma of burned hair and flesh, and blood, and gun smoke, and plaster dust. These are soon overpowered by a different stench—an acrid, chemical sort of smell like burning rubber or perhaps melting plastic. Mrs. Carlucci takes a breath and suddenly her lungs ache. She coughs as the smell becomes stronger. Black smoke begins to roil in the space beyond the hole. She realizes that the carpet in Terri and Caleb's apartment is on fire.

"Oh dear..."

Here they went through all the trouble of stopping the crazies from setting the apartment building on fire, and now she's gone and done it herself. Worse, judging by the stench and how black the smoke is, the fumes from the burning carpet are most likely toxic.

Good, she thinks. *Maybe that will take some of them with it.*

Of course, she and her neighbors will be breathing it,

too, as will her cats.

Mrs. Carlucci holds her breath and empties the rest of the can, spraying it back and forth in a wide, sweeping motion. The lighter grows hot in her hand, burning her thumb, but she ignores the pain. Soon, Terri's bedroom is fully ablaze. The flames leap and crawl. Their speed surprises her.

A random thought occurs to her then, out of nowhere. Mrs. Carlucci is no expert on firearms. That was her husband's forte. But she thinks one of the druggies—the one who jumped out the window—might have had a .45, the same as her. If so, she could have gotten some ammunition from him.

The pain in her thumb is almost unbearable now. The spray sputters, and then dies. Satisfied that the horde won't be able to crawl through the hole, Mrs. Carlucci tosses the empty can through the hole. It lands among the flames and rolls twice before coming to a stop. Then she picks up the two spare aerosol cans and hurries to the hallway. She finds Sam hunkered down against the wall, hidden in the darkness. Only his coughing gives him away.

"What's that smell?" he asks.

"The complex is on fire."

The living room door begins to splinter and crack. The hinges buckle with a torturous shriek. Mrs. Carlucci tastes smoke in the back of her throat.

"I think Tick Tock and his friends must have found another axe," Sam whispers, raising the pistol. "You'd better go with Stephanie and Terri."

"Nonsense. I'm staying right here. I can get more with flame than you can with bullets. How many do you have left, anyway?"

"Not many," Sam admits.

There is a short, muffled explosion behind them. Sam jumps, nearly dropping his revolver.

"What the hell was that?"

"Relax," Mrs. Carlucci reassures him. "It was just my empty can of hair spray exploding."

The top hinge on the living room door breaks free of the wall. The door shudders. The battering grows frenzied.

"Girls," Mrs. Carlucci shouts, "you'd better hurry!"

The only response is the sound of the axe striking the wall—nearly lost beneath the cacophony on the other side of the door. Black smoke curls out of Stephanie's spare bedroom and down the hall. Mrs. Carlucci's eyes begin to sting. Coughing, Sam pulls his shirt up over his nose and mouth. Then he repositions himself again, gun pointed at the door. Mrs. Carlucci notices that his hands are shaking.

She readies another can of hairspray and the lighter, and realizes that her hands are trembling, as well. Tears roll down her face, and not all of them are caused by the smoke.

Please Lord, she silently prays, *I've been your good and faithful servant for how many years now? Too many to count. Please keep my cats safe and see them through this night. And please keep my neighbors safe, too. Watch over us all, and protect us with your blood, which was shed for us. Especially Caleb. He's just an innocent. He doesn't deserve this horror. Please...*

As the smoke gets thicker, Mrs. Carlucci realizes that the hallway is growing noticeably hotter.

Sixteen

Hannibal, King, Queenie, and Princess: Apartment 4-D

Hannibal knows fear. He is no stranger to it. Indeed, he has known it his entire life.

He remembers when he was a kitten, born in an abandoned shed in the middle of a swamp near the Susquehanna River bottoms, and how fear crept into that shed each night, no matter how tightly he snuggled against his mother's warmth, or burrowed between his brothers and sisters. He remembers the terror every time his mother left the den, and how that fear solidified on the day she didn't come back. He remembers the horror he felt when he found her, caught in a hunter's trap, dead of blood loss after trying to gnaw her own leg off in an effort to free herself and return to her litter. He remembers nuzzling her, trying to get her to wake up, and not understanding why she was so cold or why she wouldn't move. He remembers staring into her sightless eyes, and how the fear gnawed at him then, chewing his belly as surely as his mother had chewed her own leg.

Hannibal remembers the panic that overwhelmed him when he ventured out on his own, wandering through the forest and the swamp, and the rain. He recalls the trepidation he felt when he first encountered the humans who would eventually adopt him—Ward, Valerie, and their daughter Ellie. And even once he lived among them, and had been accepted into their family, he still felt fear—fear that he would lose them, too. Fear that they might cast him back out into the wild. Fear that he was unworthy. It was that fear that had driven him to earn his keep, bringing back trophies on a daily basis—mice, voles, snakes, frogs, butterflies.

Anything he could catch, he brought it back to show his gratitude and keep his place. And his gifts had been accepted and appreciated and rewarded with scratches under the chin and more food and a warm place to sleep.

But in time, a new fear settled upon him—a fear that he might lose his adoptive family through other means. Fear that something might happen to them, that something might harm them, and that he wouldn't be able to defend them from it.

And eventually, that was just what happened. He had tried to protect Ward and Valerie and Ellie, especially Ellie. And for a while…well, for a while, he had protected them. But then…

Ultimately, he had failed. And in failing, he lost them, and became lost himself once again.

Now, Hannibal has this new home, and this new family, and—until tonight—the fear had subsided a bit. He likes Mrs. Carlucci well enough. She feeds him, and gives him water, and pets him when he deigns to let her. What more can a cat ask for, really? There's a good spot on top of the recliner in the living room. It's his spot and he has marked it as such. He likes to lay there during the day, when the sun streams through the window. He is strictly an indoor cat now, and he misses chasing things and hunting, but his benefactor has an assortment of catnip filled toys that suffice when the mood strikes him. He is not overly fond of King, Queenie, and Princess. They are pampered and fat and have never spent a day outside. Born in captivity, raised in captivity, and it has never occurred to them to yearn for more. And why should they? Food and comfort and shelter are here, and they don't know they are missing more than that. They have never rutted beneath the moon or rolled in dew-covered grass or stalked a bird. They are soft. Plus, they weren't very nice to him when Mrs. Carlucci first brought him home from the shelter. They showed their displeasure by alternately hissing or ignoring him. But Hannibal is indifferent to the other cats.

What he is not indifferent to is fear. It hangs thick in the apartment complex tonight—an almost palpable thing. Hannibal can hear it, smell it, see it, and taste it. It makes his fur stand up and his whiskers twitch and his sphincter tighten. If he still had testicles, they would probably be tight right now. His tail swings back and forth, snapping like a whip.

All four cats are in the bedroom. King, Queenie, and Princess are cowering beneath the bed. They peer out at him from the darkness, terrified, but Hannibal pays little attention to them. He paces back and forth along the far wall. He hears Mrs. Carlucci, she who feeds and scratches him, on the other side of that wall, along with another sound—a noise like somebody striking the wall. It frightens him, but not nearly as much as the other things he is hearing—the screams, cries, gunshots, and shouts. There's another noise, too. A crackling, hungry sound. He remembers that sound from his previous home. He heard it every time Ward burned something in the stone pit in the backyard. The sound is fire.

Of all the things Hannibal fears, fire scares him the most.

From the bedroom, King, Queenie, and Princess meow as one. Their tones are plaintive and frightened. Hannibal responds with a meow of his own, trying to sound brave, and failing.

Hannibal's ears swivel as he detects a new sound—a rustling noise at the front door of the apartment. He furtively pads down the hallway, cautiously looking around the corner. Yes, there is somebody at the front door. Several somebodies, judging by their smell. Hannibal doesn't like their scent. They smell...wrong. Not like other humans. Indeed, their scent is unlike anything he has ever encountered.

Hannibal's fear grows, gnawing inside of him, just like

it did that day he found his mother. He fights to control it, struggles not to flee back into the bedroom and cower in the dark with King, Queenie, and Princess. Digging his claws into the carpet, he ducks low and slinks forward again, entering the living room. That strange scent is stronger now, and he senses more people arriving outside.

Then, something slams against the door, startling him. Hannibal holds his ground, but his haunches are raised and his eyes are wide. His ears go flat against his head, and he tucks his tail between his legs. The door is slammed again. Hannibal hisses, baring his teeth in warning. Another barrage shakes the door. The doorknob—that cursed device which he has never been able to master—rattles. Hannibal backs up one step. Then two. Then three.

The door bursts open, and Hannibal's resolve breaks. He darts to the left, slipping into the narrow space between the couch and the wall as six figures rush into the apartment. Their scent is overwhelming, and it is all Hannibal can do not to yowl in horror. Even worse are the sounds they make, and the way they move. They are more like a pack of animals than humans, and the behavior simultaneously fascinates and terrifies him.

He remains hidden behind the couch as they search the apartment, hurriedly going through the kitchen and the living room, and yanking open the hall closet door. He feels an overwhelming sense of rage and territoriality when one of them paws the recliner, soiling his favorite sunning spot, ruining it with their stink. But the rage quickly dissipates, and the fear returns. Hannibal's heart beats faster, and he curls himself into a ball as one of them inspects the couch.

Then, just when he can't take it anymore, just when he is about to howl and hiss and come out slashing and biting, the figures move on, disappearing into the bedrooms. There is silence, for a moment, and then Princess shrieks. The agony and terror in that wail momentarily paralyzes him. Princess's howls are cut short, and then King begins to cry, as well. He hears paws scrabbling on the carpet, and feet pounding after them in pursuit, and although he can't see it, Hannibal hears it when Queenie is caught and repeatedly smashed into a wall. He hears her bones snap. Her howls are the briefest, but also the most intense.

Hannibal eyes the open door, and the darkness beyond it. He is torn between his loyalty to Mrs. Carlucci and his fear.

In the end, it is his fear that wins.

Hannibal slinks out from under the couch and darts toward the door. He slips outside, paws slapping across the hard asphalt of the parking lot, and runs for the safety of the nearby woods. The last thing he sees before he disappears into the tree line is an enormous, overweight man. The man is like the others—a human but not a human. He is bestial and cruel and his scent is the worst one of all. It seems to roll off the figure in great waves.

And then, for the second time in his life, Hannibal returns to the wild, leaving behind the dangers of civilization.

Seventeen

Grady, The Exit, and Shaggy: Apartment 6-D

"So that was you, banging on the ceiling?"

Grady nods, struggling to catch his breath as he, Mendez, and their new arrival—the druggie from next door—hastily restore the barricade over the front door. He never liked this kid, or his roommate, even before tonight, and his demeanor over the last few minutes hasn't given Grady any reason to reassess his feelings on the matter.

"What did you say your name was again?" he asks.

"Shaggy."

"Right. Shaggy. Yeah, that was me, banging on the ceiling. We were trying to signal you."

"For what?"

Before Grady can respond, Mendez interrupts.

"How many of you were still alive up there?"

"I don't know. There was me, Turo, the writer guy, the he-she, that old lady from upstairs. Oh, and this fine mom with her kid. But Turo…he…" Shaggy shrugs, and his eyes flick to the floor. "There's five now. Or, at least there was when I left."

"And how many attackers?"

"A lot more than five. I mean, like there didn't seem to be no end to them. And that fat fuck, he was the worst."

"Fat fuck?" Grady frowns.

"Yeah, some big motherfucker with a Hello Kitty tattoo on his floppy fucking man-boob."

"I don't know what that is," Grady replies.

"You don't know what man-boobs are?"

"No, that kitty thing. I don't know what that is."

"I saw him, too," Mendez says. "Just a glimpse, when I was driving through the parking lot. It seemed to me like he was leading them."

"Yeah," Shaggy agrees. "I think he is."

Mendez pauses, his brow creasing.

"What are you thinking, Mendez?" Grady asks.

"I'm wondering what happens if we eliminate him," Mendez says. "The fat man. If he's out of the picture, how might the others react?"

Shaggy chuckles. "Some alpha male shit?"

Mendez nods. Judging by his expression, Grady is fairly certain that he doesn't think much of their other neighbor, either.

Shaggy points at the door. "So, like, that's your car outside?"

Mendez nods again. "It is. Although judging by what you've told us, I doubt we're going to drive it out of here."

"For real. Your car is fucked up, dude."

"And which way is the fire spreading?" Grady asks.

"Everywhere," Shaggy replies. "Depends on which way the wind is blowing."

Mendez slides the final piece of furniture into place. "Do you think it will reach the building?"

"Better hope not. There's a full gas can on your car."

"And a full tank in the car," Mendez responds. "That would be unfortunate."

"Unfortunate?" Shaggy laughs. "Yeah, you could fucking say that."

Grady steps back from the finished barricade and wipes his hands on his pants. Then he turns to them. "So, what are we going to do? We can't drive out. The yard is on fire. Our luck's not going to hold out much longer."

"The back window," Mendez tells him. "I still think that's our most feasible route of escape. If what Shaggy says is true, then the numbers in the parking lot must have thinned by now. It sounds like most of them are in the building, now."

"What about the backyard? From what Shaggy says, and from the brief glimpse I got when I opened the door, there are a lot less of them out there now."

"Do you want to risk running through the fire?"

"No, but maybe we could run around it."

"I'd rather go for the window and the parking lot," Mendez says.

Grady still has major misgivings about this plan, but he can't think of anything better, other than staying put, so he doesn't argue.

Shaggy winces, holding his side.

"You okay?" Grady asks.

"Not sure. Fucked myself up pretty good when I fell. I think I might have broken a rib or some shit. And I scratched my back up, too."

"If you have a broken rib, then you shouldn't be moving around."

"Well, it ain't like I'm gonna just sit here and wait for them crazy fucks to kill me. I gotta keep moving. And besides, I owe the fat boy for Turo. That debt ain't paid."

"You keep moving around and the broken rib could puncture something," Grady insists. "I saw it happen in the war."

"I'll be alright."

"Suit yourself." Then, something else occurs to Grady. He turns to Mendez. "If Shaggy's group were able to dig through the walls, then what's to stop the nudists from tunneling through the floor upstairs to get to us?"

"Nothing," Mendez replies. "Which is all the more reason why we can't stay here, in hiding."

"The dude upstairs said the floor and ceilings have a lot thicker concrete than the walls," Shaggy tells them.

"Regardless," Mendez replies, "we need to go. If you hadn't shown up when you did, Grady and I would have been out of here already."

"I don't know about that," Grady disagrees. "There were still a lot of them out in the parking lot."

"Yes, but their numbers are thinning. I suspect they will fluctuate all night. That's why we should wait by the window, and be ready to go at a moment's notice."

He turns and walks down the hall. Grady follows him. After a moment, Shaggy does the same.

"Well, I'm with you guys," Shaggy declares. "Thanks again for letting me in. I thought for sure I was fucked."

"Don't thank me." Mendez points at Grady. "It was his idea. I didn't want to open the door, but Grady insisted."

"Oh…"

"Don't take it personally," Grady whispers. "Mr. Mendez is sort of on a mission."

"A mission? The fuck does that mean?"

"How many bullets do you have in that gun?" Mendez opens the bedroom door.

"Good question," Shaggy replies. "I'm not sure anymore. I was gonna check that earlier."

As Mendez and Grady walk into the bedroom, Shaggy pauses in the hall. He releases the magazine and turns it over in his hand.

"Good thing you reminded me. I've only got two fucking rounds left. One in the clip and one in the chamber."

"That's good," Mendez says.

Grady turns to him, confused. "That's good? How is it good?"

"He's got two bullets. If they get in here, that means he's got one for you both. Wasn't that an option for you earlier?"

"Don't start, Mendez."

"The fuck are you two talking about?" Shaggy slides the

magazine back into the gun.

"Don't worry about it," Grady says. "I've got plenty of ammunition left for mine."

Mendez's mouth twitches. "Do you have enough for every one of those people outside?"

Grady shrugs. "I guess we'll find out."

"If you do decide to shoot yourselves, remember I'm not part of your suicide pact."

"The fuck are you talking about?" Shaggy asks again.

"Mendez can't die," Grady tells him.

"That's right," Mendez confirms, smiling. "I can't. Not tonight. So let's get back to work on escaping."

Eighteen

Sam, Terri, Caleb, Stephanie, and Mrs. Carlucci : Apartment 3-D

When the door is smashed open, Sam pauses for a second, waiting for a clear shot. He takes it one breath later as the horde swarms through the door. He fires all five rounds, aiming for their center mass, and drops four naked attackers. The next wave slows, their speed impeded by the still-writhing bodies.

"Empty," he shouts.

"My turn." Mrs. Carlucci steps forward, hair spray and cigarette lighter at the ready, and unleashes a burst of flame. The crazies fall back, recoiling from the flames. For the first time, Sam sees something in their expressions other than murderous lunacy. He sees fear.

"They're afraid," he yells. "Keep it up!"

"I have no intention of stopping," the old lady assures him, pressing her attack.

She arcs the flame back and forth in a sweeping motion. Flames scorch the doorframe and the walls, turning white plaster black with soot. Too late, Sam sees the framed picture of him and Sergio lying on the floor. He wasn't even aware that he had dropped it. As the picture begins to smolder, he resists the urge to rush over and snuff out the flames. It—and the apartment complex—are already on fire. It's too late to save anything now, other than themselves. And why would he bother saving the photo, anyway? Just an hour ago, he was willing to let it all be thrown in the garbage dumpsters— willing to leave it all behind with his corpse. Why should things be different now?

What has changed, he wonders as he hurriedly reloads

147

his Taurus. Why this sudden urge to live? Why hasn't he simply put down the gun and let the mob have him? Is it because he's afraid of the pain? Afraid of being hacked to death or tortured? Afraid of being dismembered like poor Turo? Sure, he decides. That's part of it. But there are other ways to escape this terror. Why hasn't he simply finished what he started, before he was interrupted? Why not kill four more of them, and then turn the gun on himself?

He hears Caleb cry out from the bedroom, and he knows the answer. It's because he has people now. He's a part of something—something more than just himself. He's no longer alone. And these people are counting on him as much as he's relying on them.

Yes, he thinks. *I want to live, goddamn it. What the hell was I thinking before?*

"Back," he shouts, raising the pistol again.

Mrs. Carlucci steps out of the way, releasing the button on the aerosol can. She sticks her thumb in her mouth, then takes it out.

"Thanks. I could use a break. That lighter was getting hot."

A group of seven naked people hover just outside the door, afraid to come inside. It occurs to Sam that there seems to be less of them now. He wonders where the rest of the crowd has gone. Not in Terri's apartment. Judging by the smoke and the sound, it's fully ablaze. Maybe they've retreated to the woods and the alley, looking for easier prey. Or perhaps they've circled back around to the backyard, deciding to try their luck with anyone left alive in the apartments below.

Shrugging, he aims at the hairy chest of a man with a large beer belly. Sam squeezes the trigger and smiles with satisfaction as he sees the man's skin split. The target staggers, and then touches one hand to his chest. He stares at the blood on his fingers in confusion, and then falls. The other crazies retreat, just out of range.

Mrs. Carlucci says something, but Sam can't hear her over the ringing in his ears.

"What's that?"

"I said what are they doing? Why aren't they attacking?"

"I think it's the fire. They're afraid of it."

Sam lowers his weapon, grateful for the respite. His arms are numb and his hands tingle.

"Sam," Terri shouts, "we're almost through the wall."

He and Mrs. Carlucci glance at each other.

"Go ahead," Sam tells her. "I'll keep watch. Call me when they're through."

Before she can respond, they both notice movement out of the corner of their eyes. A dark shape fills the doorway. They turn toward it and see Tick Tock standing in the door. His massive chest heaves. His eyes glare, unblinking. There is blood smeared on his face, and when he smiles at them, Sam swears he sees skin dangling from between the behemoth's teeth.

"Fuck you, buddy."

Sam snaps the pistol up, but before he can take the shot, Tick Tock is gone, retreating back into the darkness. They hear a tremendous roar, and then, hesitantly, the crazies start to slink forward, approaching the doorway. They move hesitantly, obviously afraid. Then Tick Tock roars again, and they seem more determined.

"Light the carpet on fire," Sam hollers, snapping off two shots.

Mrs. Carlucci stares at him in confusion, and he realizes she couldn't hear him.

"The carpet," he shouts. "In front of the door! Light it up!"

He inhales a lungful of smoke, and begins to cough, unable to focus his aim. He bends over, retching and gagging, and waves wildly at the door.

149

Mrs. Carlucci rushes forward and sprays fire at the carpet. It catches quickly, and the living room begins to fill with choking, toxic fumes. The smoke looks oily. The flames race across the floor, licking the bottom of Stephanie's sofa and recliner. The group at the door hesitates again, shielding their faces with their arms.

Bellowing, Tick Tock stomps forward, and shoves his followers inside. They trip over the dead bodies and fall face-first into the flames. Frantic, they roll and flail, trying to push themselves upright. Sam points the pistol at them and squeezes the trigger until it clicks empty.

Tick Tock disappears again, but Sam can hear him screaming outside, even over the echoing gunshots.

Mrs. Carlucci lets loose another gout of flame. Then she looks down at Sam.

"Go…" Sam wheezes, motioning toward the bedroom.

"You're coming, too."

Mrs. Carlucci throws the can into the fire and then grabs his wrist, urging him along. Sam stumbles behind her. His throat feels like it's on fire and his eyes are watering so much that everything turns blurry. He realizes that his elderly neighbor must be having the same difficulty, because she leads him into a wall.

Recovering, they turn down the hall toward the bedroom. Sam gapes, alarmed at the amount of smoke roiling out of the spare bedroom. The heat wafting from that direction is unbearable. He coughs again, and then feels Mrs. Carlucci tugging his arm. Sam frowns, confused. Has the old woman suddenly gotten shorter? No, he realizes. She's crouched down, closer to the floor. He follows her lead and suddenly he can breathe again.

"Crawl," she gasps, pointing.

They proceed down the hallway on their hands and knees, until they find the bedroom door. Somebody has shut it, probably to keep the smoke out. Sam wonders when that happened. It must have been in the last minute. Otherwise, he wouldn't have been able to hear Terri before.

"Quit lollygagging," Mrs. Carlucci snaps. "There's no time for nonsense right now, Sam."

Nodding, he follows her as she reaches up, turns the doorknob, and crawls inside the bedroom. Once they're in, Sam slams the door behind him. This room is smoky, too, but it's bearable. Sam rises to his feet, and then helps Mrs. Carlucci stand. He glances around the room, and sees that Terri has managed to tunnel through to Mrs. Carlucci's apartment. She, Caleb, and Stephanie are standing next to the wall.

"We...we weren't sure what happened to you," Stephanie explains. "So we were waiting."

Sam nods, wiping sweat from his brow. "It's okay. You did fine, Steph."

"Did you see my cats?" Mrs. Carlucci asks, her voice thick with worry.

"No," Terri replies. "But it's quiet over there. None of the... whatever these people are...none of them are inside, yet. I'm sure your cats are safe."

"How do we know?" Sam asks. "How do we know they're not inside?"

Terri shrugs, and glances at Stephanie.

"Wouldn't they have come through the hole after us, as soon as we broke through the wall?"

"Yeah," Sam agrees. "Good point. Although...they seem to be more calculating than we thought."

Stephanie frowns. "What do you mean?"

He starts to tell her about their behavior at the door, and Tick Tock's bullying of them, but before he can, Mrs. Carlucci hobbles across the room.

"You people can stand here and talk while the building

burns down, but I'm going to see to my cats, and then we're getting out of here."

Sam smiles, encouraged at the old lady's courage and single-minded determination. She really is a remarkable woman. He hates that it's taken tonight's events for him to truly get to know her, and he resolves to make up for that mistake when things return to normal.

If they return to normal, he thinks.

Resting his back against the bedroom door, Sam flips open the .357's cylinder, ejects the empty brass casings, and fumbles in his pocket for more ammunition. His vision has cleared now, but his eyes still sting and his throat still tastes like smoke.

Mrs. Carlucci crouches down and climbs through the hole in the wall.

"Hannibal? King? Queenieeeeeeeeeeeeeeeee…"

Screaming, Stephanie, Terri, and Caleb back away from the wall as something jerks Mrs. Carlucci into the darkness on the other side. Only her legs are visible, jittering wildly.

"No!"

Sam lunges forward, gun raised, but he realizes he can't fire into the tight space without hitting Mrs. Carlucci. Instead, he grabs her ankle and pulls. Someone on the other side yanks harder, as if the old woman is nothing more than a rope in a bizarre game of tug-of-war. Then Sam spots Mrs. Carlucci's head and face. Her eyes and mouth are wide with terror. Several pair of dirty, hairy arms are holding her. Something silver flashes in the darkness—a straight razor. Sam shrieks as it is dragged across her throat. Blood jets from the wound, turning the arms of her captor's red. It splatters onto Sam's face, dripping into his eyes, but he barely notices.

Realizing there's nothing he can do, he raises the gun again and fires into the hole. He squeezes the trigger until it clicks empty. Then he scuttles away and glances at the others.

"Out the window! It's our only chance."

"But the fall," Stephanie protests.

"We don't have a choice, Steph! They're in her apartment. And yours is on fire. It's the only way out."

He runs to the window. Unlike the other apartments, this room doesn't have an air conditioner. Sam is grateful for that. He rips the curtains down, shoves the blinds aside, and unlatches the hasp at the top. Then he slides the window up. He coughs, as the breeze blows smoke into his face. Sam looks out on the backyard. Parts of it are on fire. Other sections are nothing more than smoldering ash. And still other portions seem unaffected, the grass still green—except for where it's covered in blood. The other thing he notices is that the mob has dissipated for the most part. They're still lurking on the fringes, and breaking into the other apartment buildings and terrorizing the houses across the street, but the vicinity immediately below him is clear.

"We can make a rope out of my sheets," Stephanie suggests, moving toward the bed.

"There's no time," Sam yells. "I'll go first. Then you, Steph. Terri, we'll catch Caleb once we're on the ground."

Terri nods, too frightened to speak. Sam can't blame her. His heart is beating so fast he's concerned about a heart attack.

He hands Stephanie the Taurus. "Drop this down to me. Then you jump."

Before she can respond, he turns to the window and climbs outside, first one leg, and then the other. Then, he lowers himself down until he's hanging from the windowsill by his hands. It is then that Sam discovers he is too frightened to let go. He glances down at the ground below him, and sees that he'll land on the sidewalk, in front of Phil and Beth's apartment. Then he spots a bush, just off to the left. It's surrounded by a deep layer of mulch. Shifting his weight, Sam swings to the left, trying his best to aim.

Then he lets go.

He lands in the mulch, just inches from the bush, and though the shock of impact travels up both legs, and the air rushes from his lungs, Sam is surprised to find that he's okay. He raises his hands up to the window, and sees Stephanie leaning out, holding the gun.

"Drop it," he says, waving in encouragement.

She does, and Sam catches it. The impact of the pistol striking his hand hurts worse than the landing did. He quickly shoves the weapon in his waistband and then looks back up. Stephanie has already crawled out of the window, and is hanging precariously, swinging back and forth.

"Go ahead," he yells. "You've got this!"

"Sam…"

"It's okay, Steph. You can do it."

"I know I can do it! But you need to move out of the way."

"Oh…"

He steps to the side and Stephanie lets go, dropping gracefully to the ground. She hisses, drawing breath on impact, and then looks at him, wincing.

"Ouch."

Sam steps toward her in concern. "You okay?"

"Yeah. Just stings the bottoms of my feet. I'm fine."

He looks back up to the window and cups his hand around his mouth. "Okay, Terri. It's Caleb's turn!"

The young mother glances down at them, her expression panicked. Sam notices that smoke is starting to curl through the window. He glances to the right and sees that both Stephanie and Terri's apartments are fully engulfed.

"It's going to be okay," he calls. "We'll catch him."

Terri nods. "I trust you, Sam. I trust you both. I'm trusting you with my little boy. Do you understand?"

"I do," he says solemnly.

Terri lifts Caleb to the window. He clings to her, crying, but then his eyes go wide as he sees something past her shoulder. He tries to scramble away from his mother, and nearly falls out the window. Terri struggles with him, and then dangles him over the sill, gripping the boy's wrists. Caleb kicks and wriggles.

"Hurry, Mommy! They're coming through the hole."

"Sam? Stephanie?" Terri sounds close to tears.

"We've got him," Sam shouts. "Let go!"

Terri does, and Caleb shrieks for her as he falls. Then, Sam catches him. The boy seems shocked. Sam is, too.

"I've got you," he says. "You're okay, Caleb. It's okay. I've got you."

"My Mom is still up—"

Terri lands on the bush, and tumbles over, sprawling into the mulch. Stephanie rushes over to her and takes her hand.

"Are you okay?"

"Yeah," Terri gasps, her expression clouded with pain. "Nothing broken."

Sam puts Caleb down and the boy rushes to his mother, hugging her tightly. Then, while Stephanie helps Terri to her feet, Sam glances around, surveying the yard. He sees naked figures looming beyond the smoke, but the fires seem to be holding them at bay.

"Any sign of Shaggy?" Stephanie asks.

Sam shakes his head. "Maybe they got him. Or maybe he got away. Let's do the same."

He leads them forward, sticking to the sidewalk. Terri and Caleb follow, hand in hand. Stephanie brings up their rear. All four are clustered together.

"Shit," she exclaims.

Sam pauses. "What's wrong?"

"I left the knife up there. And the hammer."

"It's okay. I've still got the gun."

He reaches into his pocket, intent on reloading, but his breath catches in his throat when he only feels four bullets. Rather than telling the others, he quietly reloads, and then snaps the cylinder shut again.

One for each of us, he thinks. *But it's not going to come to that. Not now. It's going to be okay. We're going to live. I'm going to live.*

They start forward again, approaching the abandoned car in front of Mr. Hicks's front door. Sam glances up and sees that his apartment is also ablaze. He thinks about his belongings, all the stuff he didn't want, all the things that didn't matter—the books he'd written, and the awards, and all the other crap, and he feels a strange sense of relief.

"You're smiling," Terri says. "What are you thinking about?"

"Oh, I don't know. It's hard to explain. Freedom, I guess. I feel free."

"We're not free yet," Stephanie warns.

"No," Sam agrees. "Not yet. But we're getting there."

Suddenly, the door to Mr. Hicks's apartment is flung open. Sam stumbles, surprised. He raises the pistol, but Mr. Hicks emerges, waving his own gun.

"Don't shoot," Sam yells. "It's us!"

Mr. Hicks squints at them. "Who's us?"

"It's Sam Miller, Mr. Hicks. I'm here with our neighbors."

"Miller?" Mr. Hicks's expression registers surprise. "You folks are still alive? I thought for sure you'd be—"

"Get the fuck out of the way, old man! The fucking apartment is on fire."

Sam recognizes the voice at once. Mr. Hicks moves aside and Shaggy bursts from the doorway, scrambling up over the roof of the car. He stares at them in surprise.

"I thought y'all motherfuckers would be burned up by now."

"Sorry to disappoint you," Stephanie says.

Another figure emerges from the apartment. Smoke seems to billow around him. As it clears, Sam recognizes the third person as one of the neighbors. He can't remember the man's name.

"You okay, Mendez?" Mr. Hicks asks.

The neighbor, Mendez, nods, wiping his eyes with his sleeve. "I am now. Need air."

The three climb over the car and down into the yard as more smoke pours from the apartment. Their clothes smell like smoke. Then Sam realizes that his do, as well.

"You folks armed?" Mr. Hicks asks.

"Just me, Mr. Hicks. We had to leave in a hurry."

"Call me Grady. And yeah, we left in a hurry, too. Messed up Mendez's plan for going out the front window."

"Into the parking lot?" Sam asks.

Mendez nods.

"Be glad you didn't," Sam tells them. "You would have never made it."

"I think we could have," Mendez replies, "but I guess we'll never know now. It became a moot point when they set the building on fire."

"Actually, that was Mrs. Carlucci," Sam explains.

Grady's eyes widen when he hears her name. "Edna? Where is she?"

Sam shakes his head, and glances at the sidewalk.

"Son of a bitch..." Grady spits on the pavement. "These goddamned sons of bitches."

"Why aren't they attacking us?" Mendez stares out across the burning yard. "There are less of them now, but even so, they still outnumber us. Why aren't they rushing in?"

"Sam thinks they're afraid of the fire," Stephanie says.

"That's right," Sam confirms. "I think it might be some sort of primal thing. Earlier, I noticed that—"

"I'm sorry to interrupt," Terri says, "but maybe we should get moving? The smoke's getting worse."

"I'm with you, young lady," Grady says.

"Terri," she replies. "And that's my son, Caleb."

A round of quick introductions are made amongst them.

"Okay." Sam points to the side of the building. "I vote we go that way. Stick as close to the building as we can. The proximity to the fire should make them keep their distance. When we get to the parking lot, we'll make a break for the alley or the woods, depending on which path is clearer. Shaggy, Grady—you both have guns. I'm down to four bullets. Can you lay down some cover fire when we get on the other side?"

Both men nod.

"I hope fat boy is up there," Shaggy says.

"I don't," Sam replies. "For all of our sakes."

Shaggy puffs out his chest. "If he is, you just leave that fucker to me."

Sam begins guiding them forward again, creeping toward the corner of the complex. The smoke isn't as bad here, but the heat radiating off the walls is definitely noticeable. Shaggy follows close behind, with Mendez, Terri, Caleb, and Stephanie clustered in between. Grady brings up the rear, his pistol at the ready.

As they reach the corner of the building, Sam holds up one finger, indicating silence. He glances back to make sure they all understand. Each of them meet his gaze, and at that moment, Sam feels prouder than he's ever been about anything in life. The look they give him is trusting, and the emotions it stirs up inside him are better than any amount of awards or good reviews. Smiling, he wipes his sweaty palms on his pants and readjusts his grip on the Taurus. Then he slinks around the corner.

Something punches him in the chest.

Stunned, Sam looks down and sees a length of rebar sticking out of him. The other end is in the hands of a naked man. Judging by the attacker's physique, he was a bodybuilder before he became a raving maniac. The weightlifter grins, and shoves the rebar deeper into Sam. Sam tries to speak, tries to warn the others, but his throat seems full of something. He raises his head, and sees two dozen more crazies creeping along the side of the building. Behind them, smiling broadly, is Tick Tock. The giant spreads his arms as if to say, '*What took you so long?*'

"Hey, fat boy!"

Suddenly, Shaggy is standing beside Sam, firing his Kimber. The first bullet hits a woman in the neck. She staggers, takes a few steps forward, and then slumps against the wall, spraying it with blood. The second round strikes Tick Tock in the stomach. The big man grunts, pauses, and then continues plodding toward them. Shaggy pulls the trigger again and again, but he doesn't seem to realize the gun is empty. Sam tries to explain this to him, but when he opens his mouth, he vomits blood.

"Motherfucker!" Shaggy stares at the weapon in disbelief.

Sam is aware of Terri and Stephanie screaming his name, but he can't turn his head to see them. He raises the pistol slowly, hand trembling, and shoots his opponent in the face, pulverizing much of the man's lower jaw. The bodybuilder doesn't seem to realize he is shot, at first. His tongue lolls out of his mouth, dangling into the gore where his chin and teeth used to be. Sam drops the pistol, grabs the rebar, and shoves forward, knocking the man over.

"Come on," Mendez yells. "Shaggy, there's too many! You'll get another chance."

"But Sam," Terri protests.

"There's no time! Run!"

Sam tries to raise his arm and wave at them, reassuring

them that he's okay, but his body doesn't want to cooperate. Despite the heat baking off the burning complex, he suddenly feels very cold.

The rest of the mob race past him in pursuit of the others. Sam wishes he could stick out his leg and trip them. He wonders where his pistol has gone. Didn't he just have it a second ago? There should be three bullets left.

Tick Tock strides up to him and grabs the rebar. He grins as Sam's blood runs down onto his hands.

"You...stink..." Sam spits more blood, hocking a big wad of it on the fat man's tattoo. Sam watches as it trickles downward. It looks like Hello Kitty is crying blood. Then, he glances back up at his opponent.

Tick Tock's smile vanishes. His knuckles pop as he grips the rebar tighter. Then, with one savage motion, he yanks it free. Sam topples over onto his side.

He wonders if he left his computer on.

He wonders if he remembered to save the story he was working on. If so, it should be in his Dropbox account when he wakes up again.

He wants to call for Sergio, but he can't breathe.

Then, a shadow covers him. Sam's eyes dart upward, and he sees Tick Tock looming over him. The behemoth has the rebar raised over his head like a spear.

Then it comes rushing down toward Sam's face.

Sam's last thought before dying is, *'But I wanted to live...'*

PART THREE

MOVING
OUT

Nineteen

Grady, Stephanie, Terri, Caleb, Shaggy and The Exit : Cranbrook Road

They've made it across the yard—dodging the flames and smoke, and staying ahead of their pursuers—and onto Country Club Road when Grady's chest pains return. The spasms are stronger this time, as if Tick Tock himself has grabbed hold of Grady's heart in one meaty fist and is squeezing it tight. Since he's got the only weapon, Grady has been bringing up the rear, picking off the crazies when he gets a shot. Now, he stumbles on his bad ankle, wheezing for breath.

"Dude." Shaggy falls back, running alongside him. "Give me the gun."

"Hell no," Grady pants. "I'm not…giving you…"

"Your face is turning gray and you look like you're about to keel the fuck over. Give me the fucking gun and let me get them off our ass. I'm out of bullets."

Grady is in too much pain to argue. He slows down enough to surrender his weapon, and then Shaggy spins around, takes aim, and drops two targets.

"Here," Grady gasps, reaching in his pocket for more bullets.

Shaggy holds out one hand. Grady nearly drops the ammunition as he places it in the younger man's palm. Shaggy hurriedly reloads.

"Get going, Mr. Hicks. I got this."

Nodding, Grady jogs after the others. It is an effort just to keep his legs moving. His feet feel like they're bags of cement, and his wounded ankle is throbbing again, despite Mendez's earlier triage. The pain in his chest begins to radiate, spiraling throughout the rest of him.

163

Mendez is at the front of the procession, leading them up a hill. Grady is surprised to see that he's carrying the young boy—Caleb—on his shoulders. For a moment, Grady wonders if his odd-duck neighbor is starting to soften. The he realizes Mendez is probably only doing this to either keep the boy quiet or to ensure that he doesn't slow them down. The boy is hunched over, clinging tight to Mendez's head. Caleb's mother is right behind them, along with the pretty girl from upstairs. She introduced herself before, but Grady can't remember her name. Stephanie, maybe? Yes, he thinks that's it. Their feet echo on the sidewalk, a counterpoint to the jeers and snarls of the mob chasing after them.

The Pine Village Apartment Complex is on their left as they run up the hill. Grady is stunned to see that their building isn't the only one on fire. Both the A and C buildings are also engulfed in flames. Despite the pain coursing through him, he feels a sudden emotional loss, as well. He thinks about all the things he can't replace—photographs from his childhood and the war, and of his daughter growing up. Gone now, and he will never get them back. Grady has renter's insurance, but some things are irreplaceable.

To their right is a suburban housing development—rows and rows of identical ranch-style homes, right across Cranbrook Road from the Pine Village Apartment Complex, yet financially unreachable. Many times Grady has sat outside his apartment of an evening, smoking a cheap cigar and watching the sun go down and listening to his aluminum lawn chair squeak, and he has stared at those houses. They were always a reminder that, despite his best efforts in life, they were something he would never be able to achieve or obtain. He imagines many of his neighbors felt the same way.

The homes in the development are occupied by white and black families, all upper middle-class, mostly white collar; the majority of them two-parent households with two or three kids and a dog. And despite the fact that their houses are located in Red Lion, none of them live in town. Not really. In the morning, the parents commute off to work—most to either Baltimore, Harrisburg, or Lancaster, a few as far afield as Washington D.C. or Philadelphia—while their children go off to private schools. They are only home at night. Weekends are spent commuting back to those same cities they work in, to shop at an Amish Market or go to a museum or to attend an Orioles game. The only time people like Grady see them is if they're outside, washing their BMW in the driveway, or once a year when they host a community yard sale, or maybe during the Fourth of July fireworks display over the high school's football field. They aren't part of the community. They aren't neighbors. They're just drones.

And now, they're prey. Grady notices that many of the houses have broken windows and battered down doors. A few of them are on fire. There are overturned cars in driveways and on the streets. Blood stains a sidewalk. A pile of still-steaming intestines slowly slops off a curb, dripping down into a sewer grating. He hears screams deeper in the development, down a side road. Then he starts to see the bodies. It's only two or three at first, lying dead in their yards or driveways, but as they reach the top of the hill and Mendez leads them deeper into the development, the corpses begin to multiply.

Tick Tock and his legions have already been here.

Grady has a sudden, intense vision of naked homicidal maniacs going door to door, shouting Trick or Treat and singing Christmas Carols while they shoot and stab and bludgeon the neighborhood.

Six shots ring out in quick succession behind him. A moment later, Shaggy is trotting beside him, fingers deftly reloading the pistol as they run.

"You gonna be okay?"

Grady nods. His mouth is too dry to speak.

"Don't be having a fucking heart attack," Shaggy warns. "I ain't carrying your ass."

Grady points behind them, indicating to the younger man that he should watch their backs.

"Don't sweat it," Shaggy says. "Ain't no more of them back there, dude. I guess fat boy couldn't keep up. He was fucking shot. Maybe that slowed him down. Some of the others split off. And I popped the rest."

Grady risks a glance over his shoulder and is surprised to see that Shaggy is telling the truth. He swoons, and stumbles, and his vision starts to narrow. Despite his protestations to the contrary, Shaggy reaches out and grabs Grady's arm, supporting him.

"Yo, Mr. Mendez! Wait up. Grady's hurting."

Mendez stops, turns around, and puts a finger to his lips, hushing Shaggy. Then, after glancing around to make sure the coast is clear, he hurries back to them. Caleb bounces atop his shoulders. Terri and Stephanie gather round Grady, as well. Grady is crouched over, gripping his knees. He's worried that if Shaggy lets go of him, he might fall over, but he doesn't want the others to worry.

"I'm...okay," he insists. "Just...out...of breath."

"There's a swimming pool over there." Mendez points. "We can hide in it for a bit. Let's hurry, though. The power's out and the streetlights are dark. I don't see any of them around, but that doesn't mean they're not out there, hiding in the shadows. I find it hard to believe they would have given up on us so easily."

"Easily?" Shaggy laughs. "Shit, wasn't nothing easy about it. We've been outsmarting them all fucking night."

Ignoring him, Mendez clasps Grady's hand and squeezes. "Can you make it that far?"

Grady is momentarily taken aback, touched by the

concern he hears in his neighbor's voice. Swallowing hard, he nods.

"I can…make it."

"Okay, then." Mendez lets go of Grady and straightens up. "We'll head for the pool. Everyone keep an eye out. Be ready to run if we encounter any of them between here and there."

"And where do we go if that happens?" Terri asks.

"Whichever way is the clearest. Shaggy, how is your ammunition?"

"Running low."

Nodding, Mendez hurries toward the house with the swimming pool. The others rush along behind him. Terri and Stephanie support each of Grady's arms. Both women smell heavily like smoke. Grady supposes that he does, as well. He feels grimy, covered in dirt and sweat and other people's blood. Feeling self-conscious, he tries to remember if he put deodorant on today. He supposes most men his age would be embarrassed by this, but Grady is grateful. Stephanie reminds him a little bit of his daughter—she has that same spunk and spirit. Heart, is what the young people call it. She has heart. He's glad for that. Heart is what will help them make it through this night.

As they sneak through the yard, Grady spots a dead dog, split down the middle so severely that the carcass is almost cut in half. The poor beast's innards are scattered throughout the grass.

"Careful," Grady warns. "Watch your step."

The pool is an above ground construct, encircled with a deck fashioned out of oak planks. A chain link security fence surrounds it. Mendez quietly lifts the latch on the gate, and glances around one more time.

"I'm going to put you down now, Caleb," Mendez tells the boy.

Caleb doesn't protest, and takes his mother's hand. Mendez leads them inside, and Shaggy closes the gate behind them. Then, crouching down, they creep across the deck. The planks creak beneath their feet, and Grady stiffens, expecting a naked person to burst out of the darkness. Instead, they reach the edge of the water without incident. Although, judging by the far-off sounds of gunshots, shouts, and screams in the distance, the crazies are hard at work throughout the rest of the town.

"So, what now?" Stephanie asks.

Mendez pulls his wallet from his pocket, drops it on the deck, and then slips into the pool. The water level comes up to his chest.

"Now, we hide out for a bit. Catch our breath. And figure out a plan."

Shrugging, Stephanie starts to take her shoes off.

"I wouldn't," Mendez says. "If we have to flee, you might not have time to put them back on."

"Good point."

She sits down, puts her legs in the water, and then slides in beside Mendez. Terri and Stephanie help Caleb into the water, and he clings to the side, paddling his legs. Terri follows, and then Grady. He pauses only to remove his wristwatch—a retirement present from his former employer. His arthritis flares as he clambers into the water, and his ankle still hurts, but the pain in his chest has subsided again, and Grady considers this a fair trade. The water is surprisingly warm. Grady finds it soothing. He sighs.

Shaggy kneels down on the deck, watching them apprehensively.

"Come on in," Grady whispers. "The water's fine."

Shaggy shakes his head. "No, I'm good."

"Don't be ridiculous," Mendez says. "Get down here before somebody sees you."

"Don't tell me what to fucking do. I'm okay right here."

"Is it your ribs?" Grady asks.

"No, they're feeling better. But I'm staying up here."

"Shaggy…" Terri speaks to him in the same tone she does her child. "Please. You're going to give us away. I'm tired and scared. Caleb is, too. We all are. We just need to rest for a few minutes. Please come in the water."

"I can't."

"Why not?" Stephanie asks

"Because…" Shaggy pauses for a moment, and glances down at the deck, refusing to meet their eyes. "Because I can't fucking swim."

"You're taller than Mendez," Grady points out, "and the water only comes up to his chest."

Shaggy glares at him.

"Shaggy, listen," Grady continues, trying to sound sympathetic. "Think about all the shit you survived tonight. Think about the odds. And yet, here you are, still standing. Now, after all of that, are you really going to let a little thing like not swimming stop you?"

Shaggy shrugs again, and then glances over the edge of the deck railing. "I don't know. What if I fucking slip or something?"

Before any of the others can respond, Caleb speaks up.

"You can hold on to the side with me, Mr. Shaggy. I'll keep you safe."

Shaggy stares at him for a moment, unblinking. Then, he slowly smiles.

"You got fucking balls, kid."

Grady sees Terri grimace in disapproval, but she says nothing as Shaggy empties his pockets, puts the gun down on the deck, and then dips his legs in the water, up to his knees. Grady notices that his lip is quivering.

"It's okay," Stephanie encourages him. "Just slip in nice

and easy until your feet touch the bottom."

Trembling, Shaggy eases himself into the water. The others gather around him in support. When he touches the bottom, he stands there, shivering. Then he laughs.

"Well, fuck me. Look at that. I'm in the pool." He turns to Caleb. "And you ain't gonna let me drown, right?"

Caleb giggles. "I promise."

Grady glances at Terri again, and sees that she's crying. He pats her shoulder offering comfort.

"It's good to hear him laugh," she whispers.

"Okay," Mendez says, his tone hushed. "I think we're safe here, for the time being. With the electricity out, there's no streetlights, and it's pretty dark in this yard. Just remember to keep your voices down, and no splashing. Agreed?"

They all nod in unison.

"Well, then." Mendez offers a tight-lipped smile. "We should discuss our options. Obviously, we can't hide out here all night."

"Why not?" Grady asks. "I mean, as long as we're quiet, we could last here until dawn."

"And what happens when the sun comes up?" Mendez points out. "Something tells me this situation won't be resolved by then. As soon as it is light out, anybody passing by will see us. We'd be sitting ducks."

"What about the borough's municipal building?" Grady suggests. "They've got a fallout shelter in the basement. We could hole up there. Wait for the police or the National Guard to get things under control."

"Shit." Shaggy bounces up and down, apparently getting over his fear of the water. "If they were going to do something, wouldn't it have happened by now? Where the fuck are they?"

"I don't know," Grady admits. "And that's the problem— we don't know anything. We don't know what's causing this, or how far it's spread, or what the government is doing to stop it."

"Government ain't gonna do shit," Shaggy insists. "Every time there's some big emergency like this, the government are the last motherfuckers to come in and help."

Mendez nods. "I agree. We can't just sit around and wait to be rescued. That's how people die. And I'm not dying tonight. The municipal building sounds like a good choice, provided we can gain access to the fallout shelter."

"It's a long walk," Grady points out.

"Only ten blocks," Stephanie says.

"Sure," Grady agrees, "only ten blocks, but that's ten blocks of crazy assholes trying to kill us."

"Point." Stephanie nods. "How about the high school? They've got an emergency shelter in the basement, too, and that's a lot closer than the municipal building."

"But we'll still be in danger on the way there," Terri points out. "Wouldn't it be better to steal a car, and get out of town?"

"That's a possibility," Mendez agrees, "but where would we go?"

"I don't know." Terri shrugs. "The woods?"

Mendez shakes his head. "The woods next to the complex was full of crazies."

"Well, there's other woods around. Or maybe one of the farms outside of town. Those backroads between Red Lion and New Bridgeville and Windsor are full of farms. Or we could go to LeHorn's Hollow. They'd never find us in there!"

Shaggy visibly perks up. "Yeah, that's what I'm talking about."

"LeHorn's Hollow?" Grady asks.

"For real. Those woods are plenty deep, even after the forest fire from a few years back. Motherfuckers would never find us in there. You can get lost in those woods."

171

Stephanie's expression seems troubled. "I've heard some weird stories about that place. Isn't it supposed to be haunted?

"Tell you what," Shaggy says, "I'd rather take my chances with ghosts than these crazy fucks. I vote we go there."

"Do you know how to hotwire a car?" Mendez asks.

Shaggy's expression sours. "What—you think I'm a thug just because of the way I dress and talk?"

"You are most certainly a thug," Mendez responds, "but I'm not judging you in the least. We need a thug on our side right now. So, do you know how to hotwire a car?"

Shaggy's shoulders sag. "No."

"Then the farms and LeHorn's Hollow are out. We would never get there on foot, and certainly not before daybreak. The more I think about it, the more I like Stephanie's idea. I suggest we head for the high school, and we should do so now, while we've still got the darkness on our side."

Grady shivers. "That's a creepy way of putting it."

Mendez climbs out of the pool. His wet clothes clinging to him and water streams from his body.

"Trust me, Grady." He reaches down and offers a hand to Caleb. "There are far worse kinds of darkness out there in the universe. Be glad that this one is our friend."

Twenty

Mike and Bryan: Speedy Stop Convenience Store, 282 Main Street

"Five years of sobriety down the fucking drain."

Mike watches Bryan tip the whiskey bottle to his lips and take a deep drink. The older man shivers as he gulps, and closes his eyes as if in bliss. When he opens his eyes and lowers the bottle, Mike notices that he's crying.

"Ah." Bryan wipes his mouth with the back of his hand. "I'd forgotten. I mean, you never truly forget. Not really. But still…"

"What," Mike whispers, "the taste?"

"No, not the taste. The kick. I'd forgotten the kick. Wish it was beer, though. An ice cold beer would be better. That's something you can taste." He sighs, hanging his head. "Five years…"

"Wait a second. You're a recovering alcoholic?"

Bryan shrugs. "I don't know about recovering. I mean, I was before tonight, but that was easy. I spend a lot of time at home, and when I'm at home, I rarely feel the urge to drink. Temptations came up from time to time, but the only time I really struggled was during social interactions with people. But now…well, I guess I'm not recovering anymore."

"I guess not."

Bryan grins. "But I *am* legendary."

Loony is more like it, Mike thinks. "But why would you break your sobriety now?"

"Come on, kid." Bryan takes another swig. "The things we've seen tonight? It's the end of the world. I might as well go out with a bang. If I'm going to slip, then this seems like the time to do it."

173

"We don't know that it's the end of the world," Mike says. "For all we know, this is some kind of local event. I think that's probably more likely."

"Well, if so, then let's just call this a momentary lapse of reason."

"Like the Pink Floyd album?"

Bryan makes a sour face. "Fuck no, not like the Pink Floyd album. I've never been a fan of them."

"Sorry."

He shrugs, studying the bottle as if an answer to their problem can be found within. "Hopefully I'll have the inner strength to stop again when this is all over—if I'm still alive."

Mike shakes his head, unsure of what to say. He doesn't want to judge this man whom he only met this evening, but he also knows they're going to have to rely on each other if they want to survive.

"So," Bryan asks, "what do you think caused all this?"

"I don't know," Mike admits. "My guess is chemical warfare or maybe something in the water. Remember all those news stories a few years back? People were taking that drug and ripping off their clothes and like breaking into houses and shit? Killing people in a frenzy."

"Yeah," Bryan says. "I remember. One naked guy in Florida bit off most of a man's face."

Mike nods. "I remember. So what if somebody put that drug in the town water supply?"

Bryan tips the bottle toward him. "Then all the more reason to drink this, instead of water. Want some?"

Mike waves it away. "No thanks. The last thing I want to be right now is drunk."

"I don't know about that. It might hurt less when they kill you if you're passed out."

"Well, I don't plan on getting killed. I just need to figure out how to get back home."

Mike lives in East Petersburg, a town across the river in Lancaster County. The only reason he's in Red Lion tonight is because he was supposed to pick up a girl for a date. Unfortunately, when he arrived at her house, the door was answered by her very angry boyfriend. Mike didn't know the guy was her boyfriend, of course. He didn't find that out until the guy asked him what he wanted and he said he was there to pick up Katie. Suddenly, there was drama and accusations and a raised fist. A very large raised fist. Mike apologized, talked his way out of it, suggested the boyfriend should take his complaint up with Katie herself, and then made a hasty retreat.

Mike has never had much luck with dating. He's good at first dates, and he has no problem finding the casual fling, but he desperately wants something more than just hook-ups and flings. But tonight, he couldn't even manage one of those.

Four blocks from Katie's apartment, he'd pulled in to a Speedy Stop convenience store for an energy drink and something to eat. Parking was almost non-existent. There were a dozen spaces outside, but twice as many cars jostling for them, narrowly avoiding hitting each other and the pedestrians walking to and from the gas pumps. He was just about to give up and find another store when the naked lady came strolling into the parking lot. Mike judged the woman to be in her mid-forties. She seemed oblivious to the commotion she was causing, as motorists and customers stopped what they were doing and gawked at her. She simply stared straight ahead, seemingly focused on the person closest to her—a man on his way back to the gas pumps, wearing shorts and a black bowling shirt.

It was then that Mike noticed the screwdriver in her hand. He didn't look at the rest of her, despite her nudity. His eyes were drawn to that screwdriver, and he watched as she shuffled toward the guy in the bowling shirt and, without a word, stabbed him in the throat.

Mike didn't see what happened next, because that was when Bryan rear-ended Mike's Saturn with his rental car. As it turned out, Bryan was from Nashville, in town on business, and had been on his way back to the airport in Baltimore. Mike staggered from his vehicle, dazed. He glanced at his car, which was now hopelessly entangled with another vehicle, and then back to the stabbing. The next thing he knew a paunchy, older man with almost platinum silver hair and wearing the loudest, most garish Hawaiian shirt Mike had ever seen was apologizing and asking about his insurance information. Mike shook his head, and pointed at the naked woman, who was now kneeling over her victim, stabbing him again and again.

Bryan said, "Holy shit!"

A customer exited the store. Mike assumed he must have had a permit to conceal and carry, because the man pulled a pistol from a holster at his side and shot the woman three times. Mike cringed, expecting the gas tanks to blow up, but they didn't. Instead, the naked lady slumped over, dead. In the aftermath, some people cried out, some hid their eyes, and most pulled out their phones and began snapping pictures of the carnage.

Then, seven more naked people came charging down the sidewalks and across the street, converging on the store. One of them had a gun, too.

And then everybody started running or dying. Mike decided that the store offered the best refuge, so he dashed toward it. Bryan followed him. Gunshots and screams fought for supremacy. Tires squealed on pavement. Glass shattered. Chaos ensued. The last thing Mike saw before dashing inside the store was a naked man smashing another man's head repeatedly into an ATM machine on the side of the building.

Mike and Bryan weren't the only customers who ended up taking shelter inside the store. There were three more, but all of them are dead now, killed by the first wave of attackers while they were still in the process of barricading the store's big plate glass windows. They repelled the rest of the attackers and finished the barricade before more could get inside. Someone had forgotten to turn off the store's sound system, and some auto-tuned pop music princess caterwauled through the speakers while they defended themselves and made preparations.

With the other three customers dead, that had left Bryan, Mike, and the store's staff—Gretta, Mark, Jorge, and Heather. Heather was a hatchet-faced woman with a nose like a knife and limp brown hair. She had rings in her ears, nose, and lip, until one of the crazies got ahold of them later, and removed them with a pair of pliers before putting the tool to work on the rest of her. Gretta was short and dumpy, and wore glasses with thick, smudged lenses. It had seemed to Mike that her expression was frozen into a permanent scowl—until the third wave of crazies broke in, and began hitting her with an axe and a crowbar. Only then had her expression changed. Mark had been about the same age as Mike—twenty-six— but still had the unfortunate acne of a teenager. The attackers had solved that problem for him when they splashed a bottle of drain opener in his face and then flattened him out on the counter and poured the rest down his throat. And Jorge— well, Jorge had kept insisting that the police would show up any minute. As far as Mike knew, he had died still believing that, shot to death while Mike and Bryan escaped unseen through a back door.

That had been their first lucky break. The mob ransacking the store had been so preoccupied with the clerks and the manager that they hadn't noticed Mike and Bryan fleeing through the storage room. The door led out behind the store, onto a fenced off concrete platform with what Mike assumed must be the building's air conditioning and heating system. There were all kinds of metal ducts, a big industrial fan, and a compressor. There was also a plastic chair, an ashtray full of cigarette butts, and several fifty-five gallon steel drums on a wooden pallet. The chain link fence surrounding the area was about ten feet high, and equipped with a sturdy gate. The section of the fence facing the alley also covered a cement block retaining wall, damp to the touch and covered with moss. The wall was high enough that Mike could just peer over the edge when standing next to it. Even better, the cluster of maple trees growing behind the store kept the entire area concealed in deep shadows. It occurred to Mike that if they successfully barricaded the door, they could hide here, crouched down behind the ducts and equipment, until help arrived.

Which was exactly what they did—quickly sliding two of the steel drums in front of the door. Both were full. Mike didn't know what of, because the labels were faded, but they were heavy. It took all he and Bryan had to move them. He was pretty sure the door would hold. When they finished, Mike and Bryan hunkered down behind the air compressor.

And now here they were.

"Where did you get that, anyway?" Mike whispers.

Bryan tilts the bottle toward the chair by the door. "Over there, under the chair. I guess some of the clerks were partying when they were out here on their smoke break. I'll tell you, Pennsylvania sucks. If this was a convenience store in Nashville, I could have snagged a six pack of beer before we came out here. But you can't buy beer in the store in this state."

"Yeah, Pennsylvania sucks for sure."

"You lived here all your life?"

Mike nods.

"What do you do?"

"For fun? Watch the tire fires on Saturday night. Seduce young Amish girls. Go to tractor pulls."

Bryan stares at him, obviously confused.

"I'm kidding," Mike says. "No, I make movies."

"What, like one of those guys on YouTube?"

"Exactly like one of those guys on YouTube. I've got my own channel."

"Oh yeah? Are you any good?"

Mike shrugs. "Well, not to brag, but I've got over ten-thousand subscribers. And I make a little money from it. Not enough to quit my job at the pizza place, but enough so that I don't struggle with the bills every month. I'm hoping that sooner or later, it leads to bigger work."

"Wouldn't you have a better chance if you moved to Los Angeles?"

"Yeah, probably."

"Then why are you still here?"

Mike sighs. He's about to explain to Bryan about his mother's fight with cancer, and how even though he has two brothers in the area, he doesn't want to leave her. But before he can do this, he hears a scuffling sound in the alley. He glances at Bryan in terror. The older man remains still as a statue, the bottle half-raised to his lips. His eyes are wide with panic. The sound draws closer—stealthy, hurried footsteps.

Bryan quietly puts the bottle down on the concrete. His expression is grim and his eyes are alert.

The footsteps draw nearer.

Mike peers over the edge of the retaining wall, and sees an Asian man dressed in burned, dirty clothes and clutching a hunting rifle. Much of the hair on his head and arms has been singed, as well. If the stranger is in pain, he gives no indication. He seems focused instead on his surroundings, his gaze darting warily from building to building, and shadow to shadow.

Bryan sidles up next to Mike and tugs his arm. "He's not naked. Think he's normal?"

Mike can tell that his fellow survivor is trying to whisper, but the whiskey is obviously impacting him. His voice carries, and the Asian man squawks in fright. He stumbles to a halt, frantically glancing around, waving the rifle back and forth. Mike then realizes that he can't see them.

"It's okay," he calls. "We're not like them. Don't shoot. You're safe."

The man squints in their direction, not lowering his weapon. "Where are you?"

"Over here, behind the store. Are you okay? You look… burned."

"I'm just singed. They set my house on fire. I almost didn't make it out, because they were tossing people off the roof of the church, and I live next door to it. But then they were having trouble hoisting this kid up, and I…"

He makes a desperate sort of whine. Mike sees his throat working, as if he's choking down a sob.

"Do you know what's happening?" Mike asks.

"A bunch of people went crazy and started killing everybody."

"Well, yeah. We know that."

"Then why did you ask?"

"I don't know," Mike explains. "I thought you might have some news. An explanation. Our phones don't have any signal."

"Neither does mine," the man confirms. "The National Guard has a perimeter set up in Dallastown. Supposedly it's right on the town limits. I'm heading there now."

"How do you know that?" Mike asks.

"I heard it on the police scanner before I lost power."

"You're welcome to hide in here with us instead," Bryan offers. "If they have a perimeter set up, then it stands to reason they'll sort things out soon. Might be less risky to just lay low."

The man shakes his head. "No offense, but for all I know, you could be like the rest of them. I'll take my chances getting there."

"If we were like them," Bryan reasons, "we would have killed you already."

The man hesitates for a moment, and then seems to make up his mind. "Even still, I'm better off by myself. Good luck to you."

"Wait," Mike pleads. "Neither one of us are from around here. How far is Dallastown?"

The man shrugs. "I don't know. Maybe two miles. You head down this alley until you get to the Rite-Aid and Hardees. Then you head up Main Street maybe another mile. Or, if there's too many of these…people in the streets, you could cut across the field behind the grocery store, instead. That's up behind the Rite-Aid. Now, if you don't mind, I've got to go."

"Hold on," Mike calls.

"I've answered your questions. I'm leaving."

"But…"

The man raises the gun and points it at the sound of their voices. "No more. Please…"

Mike starts to speak again, but Bryan reaches out and squeezes his shoulder hard. When Mike turns to him, Bryan shakes his head no. When they turn back, the man hurries down the alley and vanishes into the darkness. They wait until the sound of his footsteps fade. Then they duck back down behind the equipment and ductwork, and speak in hushed whispers.

"What do you think?" Mike asks.

Bryan takes another sip of bourbon. "About what?"

"About what that guy said. The National Guard. Do you think we should try for the perimeter?"

"How are we going to get there without our cars? I'm not crazy about walking around in the dark. We don't know this town. If one of them sees us, or if we take a wrong turn…"

"Maybe we could get our cars untangled, and take one of them. He said Main Street runs into Dallastown. Well, that's Main Street out in front of the store. It's right there. All we have to do is get a car free and floor it."

"Yeah, and you know how much noise and commotion we'd make, getting the cars free of each other? Our bumpers are entwined. It would be like ringing the dinner bell for these freaks."

"I don't think they're zombies."

Bryan shrugs. "You know what I mean."

They fall into silence after that. Mike shifts back and forth, stretching his aching muscles and joints. Mosquitoes buzz his ears and face, but he's afraid to slap at them— worried someone might hear the noise. He isn't sure how long they wait there, but it's long enough that a half dozen crazies scamper by. Five of them proceed down the alley. All of them are carrying weapons and clearly hunting. The sixth passes within feet of their hiding place, just on the other side of the chain link fence. Mike's heart races in terror when the crazed woman stops in front of the gate. She peers into the enclosure, but apparently doesn't see them. He holds his breath until she moves on.

"Fuck." Mike exhales when she's gone. "I thought she'd spotted us for sure."

"Me, too," Bryan agrees, taking another swig from the bottle.

"I changed my mind," Mike says. "Let me get some of that, if you don't mind?"

Shrugging, Bryan hands him the bottle. Mike wipes the rim with his hand and then lifts it to his lips. He shudders, grimacing as the bourbon burns his throat.

"Jesus," he chokes. "That's like drinking smoke and tree bark. I think I'll stick with beer."

Bryan nods, his expression solemn. "That was always my drink of choice."

"I shouldn't drink beer at all," Mike responds. "All the weight I've put on recently makes my t-shirts fit like sausage skins."

Bryan chuckles. "You're young. You can lose that easy. Wait until you're my age. The pounds are harder to take off."

Mike hands him back the bottle, noticing as he does that Bryan's hands are shaking. He is about to ask the older man if he's okay, when they hear more shuffling footsteps in the alley. The two of them tiptoe back to the retaining wall and peer out over the side, expecting to see more naked people.

Instead, they see a group of fully-clothed people, none of whom look the least bit insane. Bizarrely, all of them are wet. Their garments cling to them, dripping water. A middle-aged Hispanic man leads them. He is followed by an old black man who looks tired, a tall and pretty girl about Mike's age, another pretty redhead holding the hand of a little kid, and a guy who reminds Mike of the character Badger from the television show Breaking Bad—the only difference is his head is shaved down to stubble. All of them carry an assortment of makeshift weapons. Even the little boy. Clubs, pipes, lengths of two-by-fours. Only one of them—the television lookalike—has a gun. All of them glance around furtively, before creeping forward a few more steps.

"What do you think?" Bryan whispers.

Mike notices that he's slurring his words slightly.

"I think they're like us," he says. "They're not naked, and they look scared."

"You sure about that?"

Mike shakes his head. The alcohol on Bryan's breath is strong. He wonders what the man's tolerance level is.

"Well, only one way to find out." Bryan stands up, weaving on his feet.

Panicked, Mike grabs Bryan's shirttail. "What are you doing? Are you drunk?"

Bryan pushes his hand away. "No, I told you before—I'm legendary."

"I don't know what that means."

Still swaying, Bryan yells, "Hello!"

Which is when the guy with the gun spins to face them and squeezes the trigger.

Twenty-One

Terri, Caleb, Stepanie, Grady, Shaggy, The Exit, Bryan, and Mike: Speedy Stop Convenience Store, 282 Main Street

Terri is thinking about Sam, and how much he reminded her of her father, and wondering why she's grieving for this man she barely knew. How is that possible? And yet, grieve she does, right up until a voice shouts out a greeting from somewhere to her left. The group stumbles to a frightened halt. Caleb squeezes her hand. Terri squeezes back, trying to figure out where they can run to. A second later, Shaggy fires Grady's pistol. The shot seems extremely loud, and the muzzle flash leaves spots floating in her vision.

"Come on, motherfuckers," Shaggy yells, stalking toward the darkness.

"Shaggy…" Grady reaches for his arm, but the younger man pulls away.

The gunshot echoes, then fades. Shaggy points the gun toward a chain link fence. The interior behind the fence is concealed in deep shadows.

"Caleb," she whispers, "you stay behind me."

He nods as she guides him into position.

"Don't waste your ammunition," Mendez warns.

"Hold on," the voice calls. "We're not like the others. Don't shoot!"

Terri frowns. The speaker's words are slurred slightly, as if he's drunk.

"That's right," a second voice calls. "Please, don't hurt us. My friend…he's not thinking straight. He's a little buzzed."

"I'm thinking fine," the first voice counters. "And that gunshot sobered me up. I told you they were like us."

185

"Yeah, well then why did they just try to shoot us?"

"Because you scared us," Stephanie explains. "Shaggy, put the gun down."

"Fuck that. I've had it with this shit. I'll shoot every motherfucker we see."

Terri notices that Shaggy is standing taut, as if all of his muscles have turned to steel. However, despite his posture, Shaggy's body seems to vibrate.

He's having a breakdown, she thinks. *He's ready to snap.*

"I mean it," he growls, "I'm gonna start shooting every fucking person we see."

"If you start doing that," Mendez says quietly, "then I'll have to assume you're turning into one of them. We don't want that to happen, right Shaggy?"

His tone is mild, even placating, but Terri still detects a hint of menace beneath his words. Mr. Mendez gives her the creeps. He has all night long. She doesn't know why. Indeed, she barely knows him. She doesn't even know his first name, or which apartment he lived in. But there's something about the man that gives her bad vibes. She wanted to jump out of her skin when he helped Caleb into the swimming pool earlier, and carried the boy on his shoulders, but she allowed both to happen—chalking her unease up to nothing more than nerves over the situation at hand. But now, she's not so sure it *is* just nerves. The way he's watching Shaggy only solidifies her feeling of uneasiness about the man. Then she realizes something else. Mendez doesn't blink. He stares at Shaggy the way a snake would study its prey—cold, emotionless...and unblinking.

Terri is pretty sure Tick Tock has that same sort of stare. She wonders if whatever has happened to drive their antagonists crazy is now happening to Mendez. And if so, could it happen to them rest of the, as well?

"Shaggy." Grady shuffles up beside him and gently

touches his arm. "Lower the gun, son. Please?"

All of the tension seems to drain from Shaggy's posture. Without turning to look at Grady, he lowers the weapon and sighs. For some reason, the sound makes Terri feel sad.

Mendez steps toward the fence. "Who are you?"

"My name's Mike. My friend is Bryan. Don't fucking shoot us, okay?"

"Is there anyone else with you?" Mendez asks.

Before the hidden men can answer, a cry goes up from a nearby house. All of them jump, visibly startled. Terri recognizes the sound. She's been hearing it all night.

"They must have heard the gunshot," Stephanie says.

"Quick," Mike shouts from the shadows. "Hide in here. Come over to the gate!"

Terri watches as the others all glance at each other. Then, Mendez leads them forward, around the chain link fence and a retaining wall, until they reach a gate. She peers into the darkness but can't see anything. Then, a young man in a black t-shirt and shorts emerges from the shadows on the other side of the gate. He sort of reminds Terri of Randy. Then she remembers that Randy is dead, and is suddenly overcome with guilt that she hasn't grieved for him more this evening. Maybe it's the stress of the situation. Maybe she just hasn't had time to grieve. But if so, then why did she feel so sad about Sam—someone whom she'd just met?

The stranger opens the gate and urgently waves them inside. Terri guides Caleb in front of her, feeling how tense and frightened he is. She wonders what long-term effect this will have on her son, and her heart breaks even more.

"It's going to be okay, baby."

Sure it is, she thinks. *I've been telling him that all night, but it's not okay. If anything, things are proceeding to get worse. I'm lying to him. Yeah, it's to keep him calm and ease his fears, but still...I'm lying. What if they get in here? What if they find us and we can't escape? The last thing I did was lie to my son...*

"I'm Mike," the young man says. "This way. Hurry."

He motions toward a cluster of metal ducts. Kneeling between them is an older man with graying hair dressed in a Hawaiian shirt. An empty bottle of liquor lies at his feet. Terri supposes he must be the aforementioned Bryan.

They all crouch down and press close together in a tight knot. Terri smells alcohol on both Mike and Bryan. And despite their dip in the swimming pool, she smells underarms and sweat and smoke from herself and her neighbors. She desperately wants a shower. And a hot tea. But mostly a shower. She kisses Caleb on top of his head. The boy's hair also smells like smoke, but beneath that she still smells her son—that intimate scent she's known since she first held him in her arms. It's the smell of his pillow and his clothes. It lingers, and gives her hope.

Her breath catches in her throat as footsteps pound down the alley. Simultaneously, a great commotion breaks out in front of the store. Although they can't see their pursuers, they hear the now all-too-familiar growls and laughter and cries. Glass shatters, and there are a series of loud booms as somebody begins striking something metal. Someone snarls on the other side of the retaining wall, and Terri gives Caleb's hand a reassuring squeeze. His skin feels very cold, and when he squeezes back, she can barely feel it.

A group of hunters emerge from the alley and cut around to the front of the store. Terri catches glimpses of them as they pass by the fence—naked and bloody, clutching weapons, hair askew, eyes alight with a maniacal combination of fury and glee. One of them carries a severed head, swinging it back and forth like a handbag. Around the throat of another dangles a necklace of penises and ears, crudely fashioned from a length of baling twine. There is no rhyme or reason to their numbers, no common denominator among those who make up their ranks, other than their nudity and predilection for slaughter. Black, white, brown, young, old, handicapped or in perfect health—the crazies don't discriminate. Apparently their ranks are open to all, and if what she's seen so far tonight is any indication, they offer the same courtesy to their targets. She wonders about their methods—about what drives their need to destroy and slaughter. Why are they engaged in such wholesale destruction?

Because they're crazy, she thinks. *Crazy people don't need a reason to do the things they do. They do it because they're crazy. Or, at least, that's how we see them. I wonder how they see themselves. Do they perceive themselves as crazy?*

The cacophony continues from around the front of the store, but the noises in the alley are fading. Then, Terri hears a new sound—slow, plodding footsteps. Her eyes widen. When she looks at the others, she sees that their eyes have done the same.

Tick Tock's shadow precedes him. When he finally appears, it's all Terri can do not to scream. She holds her breath as he lumbers past, his greasy bulk only inches from the chain link fence. He's close enough that Terri hears him wheezing like an asthmatic tractor trailer. Drool runs down his chin. His head tilts back and forth, back and forth, like some bizarre metronome.

"I hit him," Shaggy whispers. "I know I shot…"

Mendez glares at him, forcefully holding a finger to his lips. Shaggy falls quiet.

Tick Tock pauses for a moment, his head still keeping time, and Terri is certain that he can hear her heart beating.

Then, he heaves himself forward again, moving on to join the rest of the horde at the front of the store.

"What the hell was that?" Mike mouths when he's gone.

"A friend of ours," Grady mutters, clutching his chest.

Another series of loud bangs rings out.

"I think those are our cars," Mike says to Bryan.

Bryan nods. "So much for your idea about driving to the checkpoint."

Terri notices that Bryan has a southern accent. She turns to him. "What checkpoint?"

"A guy said there's a National Guard perimeter on the outskirts of town. We were debating trying to make it there when you folks showed up."

"What guy?" Mendez leans forward, speaking in hushed tones. "When did you hear about this?"

Bryan shrugs. Terri still smells the booze on him, but his eyes seem clearer now.

"I don't know. Maybe ten minutes before you got here. A guy passed by with a rifle. He said he had a police scanner, and before the power went out, he'd heard that the National Guard had set up a perimeter in the next town over."

"Which town?" Grady asks.

"Dallas, I think?"

"Dallastown," Mendez corrects him.

"Yeah, that's it," Bryan responds. "Sorry. I'm not from around here."

A loud crash echoes from out front. It is followed by the sounds of the mob breaking into the store.

"We barricaded it earlier," Mike explains. "Sounds like they're inside again, though."

"The fat guy," Bryan mutters. "The one with the twitchy head? Is he looking for you?"

"We don't know," Stephanie admits. "Maybe. We've sort of been…on the run from him all night."

Bryan sighs. "Sounds like he's a determined son of a bitch."

Terri's eyes are drawn to Mendez. While the others

whisper or glance around fearfully, flinching at every new noise, he remains calm, appraising the situation. He stares at a nearby door which has been blocked by a fifty-five gallon drum. Then he studies the retaining wall and the chain link fence.

"I don't know if he's hunting us or not," Mendez says, "but they were obviously drawn here by the sound of the gunshot, or perhaps your shouts. It is pure luck they didn't see us hiding back here, but that will change the moment they come through that door."

"Don't worry," Mike says. "That barrel is full. It took both of us to move it. Damn thing weighs a ton. They're not getting through there."

"Then you haven't seen what we've seen tonight," Mendez tells him. "Eventually they will. We're sitting ducks here. They can trap us easily. We need to move on."

"Move on to where?" Terri has to struggle to keep from sobbing. She's afraid that if she starts crying now, she won't be able to stop, and that's not going to help Caleb's emotional state.

"Dallastown," Mendez replies.

"Are you insane?" Grady gestures angrily. "You know how far a walk that is?"

"Yes," Mendez says. "About two miles."

"On foot," Grady counters. "With however many of them there are between us and this National Guard barricade that we don't even know for sure exists."

"It beats sitting here waiting to die," Stephanie says.

Terri nods. "I agree. We can't stay here, tempting as it might be."

The sounds of destruction inside the store grow louder.

"I've been thinking," Mendez whispers. "These people haven't been attacking each other. The only time they fight among themselves is when they're in each other's way.

They're like pack animals. So, how are they identifying each other? What's the one thing they all have in common?"

"They're naked," Terri answers.

"Exactly. I think we should be, too."

"Absolutely not," Stephanie says, her voice growing louder. "There's no way."

"Keep your voice down," Mendez replies. "And on the contrary, it might be the only way. If we're naked, they might mistake us for one of them. It could save your life, Stephanie."

"No," Stephanie insists. "I'm not taking my clothes off in front of a bunch of strangers."

Terri hears the girl's voice cracking with emotion, and speaks up quickly. "Me, either. I'm not comfortable with that. And I've got Caleb to think about."

"If you're really thinking about your son," Mendez tells her, "then you'll reconsider."

Terri glares at him. Mendez stares back at her, unblinking, until she looks away.

"Okay," he says, "does anyone here have a lighter or matches?"

"I do." Bryan rummages in his pants pocket and produces a silver, stainless steel lighter with Bile Lords emblazoned on the side. "This is sentimental. The lead singer of the band gave it to me. Make sure I get it back, okay?"

"Thank you." Mendez accepts it from him. "I'll try my best. But no promises, of course."

Grady frowns. "What are you up to, Mendez?"

There is a loud crash inside the store. Terri thinks it sounds closer than the others.

"They're in the storeroom," Mike says, his tone frightened.

"See that tiny manhole cover over there?" Mendez points.

Terri looks in the direction and sees it—a small, circular cover about five feet away from the gate, embedded in the pavement.

"That's the storage tank for the gas pumps out front." Mendez begins unbuttoning his shirt.

"Wouldn't the tank be under the pumps?" Mike asks.

"No. They keep it located elsewhere as a safety precaution."

"Shouldn't you guys keep it down?" Terri asks. "What if they hear us?"

"The noise they're currently making should offer us some protection," Mendez explains, setting his shirt on the concrete and unbuttoning his pants. "But it certainly won't last. My plan is simple. You're all going to run while I blow up the convenience store."

For the first time since their arrival, Shaggy stirs. "Say what?"

Mendez nods, pulling off his underwear while still seated. The position is not flattering. Terri averts her eyes. Then, as an afterthought, she covers Caleb's eyes with her hand, which he immediately pushes away.

"Stop it, Mom. I want to know what's going on, too."

"What's going on," Mendez continues, "is exactly what I said. You guys are going to start down the alley and get as far away as you can, while I blow this place up. At the very least that will create a diversion, and we can slip away in the resultant confusion. With any luck, I'll also take out Tick Tock and most of his army. That should get them off our backs. I would guess that any other crazies in the vicinity will be drawn to the noise. That should buy us some time as we search for the perimeter."

"But how are you going to do this?" Stephanie asks.

"I'm not sure," Mendez admits. "I won't have to worry about the safety switch inside, because the power is out. But

I believe that I can get the vapors to light inside the tank itself."

"Are you going to drop my lighter down inside the tank?" Bryan asks. "I told you that was sentimental."

Mendez shakes his head. "No. Dropping a match or a lighter in there would achieve nothing. They'd be snuffed out as soon as they were submerged in the gasoline. The vapors are what's combustible. If I can get that to light, then the gasoline will catch. Depending on how much is in the tank…well, as I said, you need to make sure you're all as far away as you can get. Shaggy?"

"Yeah?"

"Since you've got the only gun, I need you to stick with them."

"But what about you?" Grady asks.

"I'll catch up. Don't worry, Grady. I told you before— I'm not going to die tonight. I can't. This is just one more way of ensuring it."

"Not if you don't have somebody watching your back," Grady argues.

"True that." Shaggy hands the gun to Grady. "Here. I'll stay with him."

"I work better alone, and the last thing I need is a babysitter."

"Fuck what you need," Shaggy says. "I owe that fat fuck and his friends for what they did to Turo."

Mendez shrugs. "Suit yourself. But understand something, Shaggy. If this goes sideways, I will not wait for you."

"Ditto."

Grady takes the weapon from Shaggy and checks the rounds. "You sure about this? Both of you?"

"I'm sure," Mendez replies.

Shaggy pulls off his shirt. "I'm sure as shit."

"Wait a minute," Bryan interrupts. "Don't Mike and I get a vote?"

Mendez begins rolling up his shirt. "No. If you prefer to wait and hide, you'll need to do it elsewhere. I have an opportunity to eliminate our enemies. I'm taking that chance."

Something hammers against the door. They all turn toward it in alarm, but the barrel remains firmly in place.

Shaggy pulls off his shorts and rummages in the pocket. Then he hands Grady a small handful of remaining bullets. "Here."

"Get going," Mendez urges. "I can't stress enough how much I think all of you should strip. But in the end, it is your choice. I'm not doing this for you. I'm doing it for me. And one other thing that just occurred to me—don't talk. We haven't heard any of them speak tonight. If you're naked, and you communicate only in grunts and cries, that may help fool them into thinking you're one of the pack."

Terri's heart hammers as more blows rain down on the door. This time, they are hard enough to make the fifty-five gallon drum wobble. Inside the store, she hears growls of frustration.

"Caleb," she whispers. "Take off your clothes. And hurry."

He looks at her in wide-eyed disbelief. "All of them? Even my underwear?"

She nods, slipping out of her t-shirt and unhooking her bra.

"And I won't get in trouble?" Caleb asks.

"No, honey. We're all going to do it."

For the first time this evening, Caleb grins. "This is going to be funny."

The others also begin to undress, casting their clothes aside after Mendez points out that carrying them might

195

reveal they aren't like the others. Only Stephanie hesitates.

"I don't know about this," she says.

Then, another series of blows rattle the door. The barrel scuffs an inch across the concrete. Swallowing, Stephanie takes off her shirt. Terri sees panic in the young woman's eyes—a different sort of fear than the kind they've faced so far tonight. Stephanie trembles from head to toe, and her breathing comes in short, desperate gasps.

"Stephanie?" Terri whispers.

When the girl raises her head, Terri sees tears welling in her eyes.

"It's going to be okay," Terri says, trying to reassure her. "I'm here with you, okay?"

Stephanie nods without speaking, and goes back to undressing. She still looks upset, but her breathing has returned to normal.

Terri feels eyes upon her as she slips out of her panties. She looks up and sees Shaggy leering, and Mike casting furtive glances in her direction. She scowls at them both. Mike turns away, blushing. Shaggy just grins. Then he turns his attention toward Stephanie. He opens his mouth, but Terri steps toward him.

"Don't," she snaps. "Whatever you were going to say, just don't."

"Damn girl. You're feisty."

"Fuck you."

Caleb gasps. "Mommy! You said the eff word."

"I know, baby, and I'm sorry. Mister Shaggy made me mad, but that's no excuse, I guess."

"Everybody ready?" Grady asks.

They nod in unison.

"Good," Grady says. "How about we knock off the bullshit?"

Terri can't help but notice how low the old man's

testicles are hanging. She supposes she's heard they do that, as a man ages, but she's never seen it before now. The sight is simultaneously revolting and fascinating. When Grady catches her eye, she quickly looks away. She glances at Shaggy again, instead. His grin grows even larger.

Grady tiptoes over to the gate, pistol at the ready, and unlatches the hasp. He slowly opens it and peeks around the corner of the fence, looking in both directions. Then he turns back to them and nods, indicating an all clear. Finally, he sneaks out into the alley, followed by Stephanie, and then Bryan.

Terri glances at Mike. He holds out his arm, gesturing for her and Caleb to go before him. Squeezing her son's hand tightly, she follows the others. Mike shuffles along behind her. She can tell he's making an effort to be quiet, but she can hear him breathing nevertheless. It sounds very loud, despite the cacophony coming from the front of the store.

Grady guides them over into the shadows beneath a row of maple trees bordering the alley. The leaves and branches rustle, swaying in the breeze as a light wind kicks up. Terri shivers. Despite it being summer, the air feels chilly on her exposed skin.

"What are we waiting for?" Stephanie asks Grady.

He nods toward the store. "Those two. I don't care what Mendez says. We're not leaving them behind."

"We could leave Shaggy behind," Terri says.

Grady chuckles. "Yeah, that boy's not right. But regardless, we can't just abandon them."

"The hell we can't," Bryan whispers. "You heard the man. He's going to blow up the store. I'm going to find a new place to hide."

Grady shrugs, not taking his eyes off Mendez and Shaggy. "If you want to go, then go. Good luck to you."

Bryan glances at Mike. "You coming?"

Mike looks at Terri. She gets the impression that he wants her to say something, but she's not sure what. His eyes have a plaintive, pleading expression. He's scared, yes. But there's something else.

When she doesn't respond, he shrugs. "Yeah. Let's go. Good luck, you guys."

"You, too," Stephanie murmurs.

Crouched low, the two men hurry down the alley. Terri sees Mike glance over his shoulder once as they flee. Then the two disappear into the darkness, as if they were never there.

Terri turns back to the rear of the store and sees Mr. Mendez and Shaggy prying open the cover to the gas storage tank. Mr. Mendez is using the length of pipe he armed himself with after the swimming pool. From her vantage point, she can almost see around the corner of the store, into the parking lot. Shadows flicker and dance on the pavement, seeming to stretch and flow, as the horde gibbers and rampages. She hears a furious, renewed attack on the store's rear service door, and glances back at Mendez and Shaggy. Mr. Mendez is holding his rolled up shirt over the flame dancing atop Bryan's Bile Lords lighter. The cloth catches fire quickly, sending puffs of oily black smoke curling skyward. Mr. Mendez holds it over the opening, letting the flames climb higher. When it is fully engulfed, he drops it down the hole and then runs. Shaggy leaps to his feet and darts along behind him.

"Oh sweet Jesus," Grady whispers.

There is a *whoomp* sound, and a brief, small flash of light. Then, just a moment later, the sound repeats, but much louder.

WHOOMP

The concrete buckles and cracks. Flames and smoke shoot up from the fissures. Mendez runs toward them, but Shaggy pauses to turn and look.

WHOOMP WHOOMP WHOOMP

The concussions spread out into the parking lot, heading toward the gas pumps. Terri has to shield her eyes as miniature geysers of flame spring up out of the pavement.

KA-WHOOMP

The ground buckles and roils beneath their feet. Terri sees Shaggy tumble backward, falling on his ass, his arms held up to ward off the fire. She spins around, shielding Caleb from the blast.

Then, a second explosion follows, and night turns to day. Terri feels a wall of heat slam into her. She tries to gasp, but all the air is gone. She can only stand their gaping, struggling for oxygen, feeling her son tremble against her. Her ears pop. Then, just when she thinks she'll pass out, the air comes rushing back in. Terri gulps oxygen, and then checks on Caleb. He looks up at her, beads of sweat running down his dirty face.

"That was cool," he says, smiling.

Terri hugs him close, and starts to cry.

"I'm okay, Mom."

Mendez dashes by, glancing at them in confusion. Terri notices that he doesn't stop or slow down.

"I told you not to wait," he gasps as they take off after him.

"You put me in charge," Grady wheezes. "I left enough people behind in Vietnam, and it's haunted me all my life. I wasn't about to leave you behind, too."

They flee down the alley, Mendez in the lead, Stephanie bringing up the rear. Terri turns when she hears footsteps behind them, expecting to see more crazies. Instead, it's Shaggy. He looks exhausted. His mouth hangs open and there are black smudges on his face, arms, and chest.

"You okay?" she calls.

He nods, gasping, and motions at them to keep running. She notices that he's holding his side.

The group draws closer together. Terri glances around, looking for Mike or Bryan, but there is no sign of them. Luckily, there's no sign of anymore naked people, either.

"Do you think they—"

"Shhh," Mendez cautions her. "No more talking from here on out. Not if we can at all help it. Remember, we want to blend in."

He slows down their pace, for which Terri is grateful. They walk in silence, alert and ready. All of them are out of breath, and Terri notices that Grady is rubbing his chest again. His expression looks pained. She wants to ask him if he's okay, but she's mindful of Mr. Mendez's warning.

The alley is a narrow lane of blacktop, bordered on both sides by backyards and garages. She bites down on her lip as stones and pebbles poke the bottoms of her bare feet. Trees rustle in the wind, and shutters creak. A rabbit darts in front of them, running for shelter. A dog howls somewhere in the distance.

Terri peers into the backyards of the homes they creep by. Some of them have clearly been broken into. Others seem untouched by the wave of violence that has decimated the town. Two of them are on fire, belching smoke and flame. Another is smoldering ruins. She sees corpses, here and there—both normal people and naked killers. A man's legs jut out into the alley. His chest has been crushed by a garage door. A woman sprawls, impaled on a white picket fence, now stained with blood. The charred remains of what she thinks might have been a child and a cat lay smoking in a backyard, amidst a circle of burned lawn. A red plastic gas can sits nearby them. The smell is revolting—the sight even worse. Caleb whimpers as they pass by it, and Terri hurries him along.

Behind them, the convenience store continues to burn. A fresh series of explosions shatter the stillness, causing Terri to jump. She assumes they can probably be attributed to the cars in the store's parking lot. She wonders if Mr. Mendez's plan worked—if he was successful in killing Tick Tock and the others.

Shaggy squeals behind her. She turns around and sees him balancing on one foot, weaving back and forth. It is not a flattering position for him, given his nudity. He glares at her, lips pressed together tightly, and points at his upraised foot. She sees a small drop of blood beading on his sole.

"Stepped on a piece of glass," he whispers.

"Sshh," Mendez hisses, not bothering to turn around.

Shaggy stops hopping, regains his balance, and shoots Mendez the finger.

They pass by a wrecked car, its front end crumpled into the side of a brick garage. The windows are smashed in, and so is the head of the young woman hanging out of the open passenger-side door. The car is making a ding sound, over and over again, indicating that the door is open, and the keys are in the ignition. A young man is scattered across the pavement nearby. One of his legs is next to the car. The other leg is sticking out of a mailbox. His upper torso has been dragged down the alley, leaving a crimson snail-like trail of gore. Terri doesn't see his head anywhere.

Then Terri gasps.

The alley intersects with another side street, from which a group of six crazies emerge. They lope into the alley, moaning and growling, carrying knives and hatchets and makeshift clubs. They pause when they see the others, heads tilted in appraisal.

Mendez growls, low in his throat. The naked people respond in kind, and begin to move on.

Terri whispers a silent thank you to a God she's not even sure until tonight that she believed in. And she's still not sure she does now, but if He will help them get through this, she promises she'll take Caleb to church next Sunday—the same promise she's been making to her mother for the past year.

Mendez leads them forward, staring directly ahead, rather than at the other group. They lope along behind him, doing their best not to appear frightened. The naked figures cut through an open yard, heading toward Main Street.

Terri realizes that she no longer hears Shaggy walking behind her. She is about to turn and check on him when he speaks.

"You have got to be fucking kidding."

All of them spin around. Terri's eyes widen in disbelief as she sees Tick Tock plodding down the alley in pursuit. One meaty fist clutches some kind of makeshift torch which sputters flame and smoke. He points at them with his other hand and roars, his head never missing a tilt. Then he starts to run, feet pounding on the pavement, rolls of fat jiggling obscenely. The flames from the torch arc out behind him.

Howling, the group in the yard charge toward Shaggy, ignoring the others. Shaggy glances at them, then back to Tick Tock, and then darts to the right, slipping into the narrow crevice between two garages. The naked people chase after him, pushing past Terri and the others without a second glance. Grady starts to go after them, but Mendez grabs his arm and shakes his head sternly.

Then, the alley is empty, except for them and Tick Tock. Terri realizes that while their disguise may have fooled the rest of the pack, it's not working on the obese giant. Trumpeting with rage, he plows toward them.

And then they run.

She hears his footfalls behind them, thundering like hooves. The sound is terrifying.

It's even more terrifying when the footsteps stop.

Terri glances back over her shoulder.

Tick Tock is gone.

Twenty-Two

Shaggy, Bryan, and Mike: The Garbage Dumpster

Shaggy grits his teeth in pain as his arm catches on a rusty nail, tearing a ragged furrow through his skin. He rips free and emerges into a fenced-in backyard. A dog charges toward him, barking furiously. It crashes into the fence and begins leaping up and down. Without slowing, Shaggy vaults the fence and dashes across the grass. The dog starts to pursue him, but is then distracted as Shaggy's pursuers follow him, clambering over the fence. Shaggy hears the animal yelp in pain, and then fall silent. Instead of glancing back, he focuses on running faster. Every loping step hurts his injured foot. Worse, his ribs and back are beginning to throb again. He ignores the pain, pushing onward.

He jumps the fence again when he gets to the house, runs along the side of it, and emerges onto a sidewalk. The sounds of pursuit echo behind him. He spots a factory across the street—the place that makes custom kitchen cabinets. He and Turo applied for jobs there once, but neither of them got hired. The fucking place never even bothered to call them back and tell them, although, now that he thinks about it, it's not like either one of them actively followed up on it either. He charges across the street, dodging a corpse, and heads into the alley next to the factory.

He is aware of the breeze on his naked skin. He wishes there was time to enjoy it.

He twists and turns, running to and fro in a panic-driven and adrenalin-fueled parkour. He leaps up onto a loading dock, ignores the pain in his foot and side, and darts around the side of the building. Then he barrels through the nearly-empty employee parking lot. Risking a glance over his shoulder, he is surprised to see no sign of his pursuers.

Maybe I gave them the fucking slip, he thinks.

He crouches down behind one of the few cars in the lot, and looks for a better place to hide or something he can use as a weapon. He doesn't see anything that will suit the needs of the latter, but he nods in approval when he sees a row of three green garbage dumpsters lined up against the factory wall. Checking to make sure the coast is still clear, he hurries, limping toward them. After reaching the dumpsters unscathed, he slowly approaches the one on the right, and lifts the lid. The hinges groan, but he barely notices, because somebody inside the dumpster swings a broomstick at his head.

Shaggy totters backward, narrowly dodging the blow. He is just about to run when the attacker gasps.

"Shaggy?"

Pausing in confusion, Shaggy peers inside the dumpster. His eyes widen in surprise.

"You're Shaggy, right? It's me, Mike. From the store. The guy you almost shot. Quick. Get in here!"

Shaggy glances around, and then hurriedly climbs into the dumpster, catching a glimpse of Bryan cowering in the back before Mike eases the lid back down, engulfing them in darkness.

"Where are the others?" Mike asks.

"Quiet," Shaggy whispers. "There's a pack of those fuckers around here. They were chasing me. Don't make a fucking sound."

The three men huddle in the dark. Shaggy tenses every time one of them moves, rustling the garbage. The dumpster's interior smells awful, and it's all he can do not to retch. Even his breathing seems loud in the enclosed space. He wonders if those crazy fuckers can hear it outside. Something buzzes in his ear—a fly. He wants to swat at it, but he's afraid to move. His fingers clench, sinking into something foul with the feel and consistency of cottage cheese. For all he knows, that may be exactly what it is. He wonders how it came to this—naked and hiding like a pussy. Hiding in garbage, no less, with two strangers he doesn't even know. He shifts his position carefully, trying not to make any noise, and his leg slides into something warm and sticky. He wonders what it could be, and then decides that he doesn't really care. The horrors of unidentifiable rotting garbage are nothing compared to the horrors outside.

His thoughts turn to Ron, and the money, hidden in that old abandoned iron ore mine in LeHorn's Hollow. It's still there, waiting for him, but Shaggy is surprised to discover that he no longer gives a fuck. He'd give up the money in a heartbeat if it meant shit would return to normal. He just wants to go back home, and chill in his apartment, and get laid, and get fucked up, and play X-Box with Turo.

Turo…

The sob wells up out of him, surprising Shaggy with its unexpected suddenness and ferocity. A weight clutches his chest, as if Tick Tock himself were sitting on it. Shaggy tries to breathe, but can only wail as another sob comes bubbling out. He begins to shake, tremors wracking his body.

"Hey," Mike whispers. "You okay?"

"Be quiet," Bryan warns. "You said those—"

Shaggy gasps for breath, unable to stop crying. He no longer feels in control of his body. It's as if his grief and shock have become palpable and sentient, playing him the way a puppeteer works a marionette. He's aware of Bryan and Mike urging him to be quiet, but he can't help it.

Then, he smells smoke.

And hears heavy, labored breathing from outside the dumpster.

Shaggy's sobs catch in his throat.

Mike whispers, "Fuck…"

The lid is flung open, and Shaggy blinks as the dumpster is suddenly flooded with light. He sees a fiery torch, but that's all. The flickering flames are oddly calming. He focuses on them, feeling his grief subside.

Screaming, Mike swings the broomstick, but it is snatched from his hand. Mike falls backward, flailing in the garbage.

Then Tick Tock leans forward and grins.

"Fuck you, fat boy," Shaggy mutters. "Go on and get it over with, you piece of fucking shit."

Mike and Bryan shriek as Tick Tock drops the flaming torch into the dumpster with them. They scurry away from it, clawing at the metal walls, as the fire begins to spread through the garbage.

"We've got to get the hell out of here," Mike screams.

He and Bryan push past Shaggy, scrabbling frantically, but the spreading flames cut them off. They circle around the other way, crawling on their hands and knees, when another crazy appears in the opening. He hands Tick Tock a plastic jug filled with some sort of yellow liquid. At first glance, Shaggy thinks it's full of piss, but when the fat man tilts the bottle and splashes the contents inside, he smells what it really is.

Gasoline.

Bryan and Mike's terrified cries turn into agonized shrieks. They scuttle away and roll around in the garbage, spreading the fire as they burn.

Smiling, Shaggy remains where he is, enjoying the feel of the heat on his skin. He glances up and sees that Tick Tock is smiling, too. His head goes back and forth, back and forth, back and forth. Shaggy's head matches his rhythm.

Then, Shaggy raises his hand and gives him the finger.

He locks eyes with the fat man, refusing to look away even as the flames come between them.

He decides he will not scream. He will not give Tick Tock the satisfaction.

He succeeds for a full twenty seconds.

Twenty-Three

The Exit, Terri, Caleb, Stephanie, Grady, and Hannibal: Main Street

The Exit tries not to cough as they walk through the smoke, but he can't help it. Although he can't see the others, he can hear them, coughing and wheezing all around him. He also knows that the smoke isn't the only reason they have stopped.

"Take hands," he rasps, deciding to risk speaking out loud. "Keep going. Don't think about it. There is nothing we can do now. It's gone."

They forge ahead, continuing down the alley. To their left is an inferno that was once the Pine Village Apartment Complex—now entirely engulfed in flames. The wind blows the smoke across the parking lot and into the alley. It occurs to the Exit that they are now where he had originally wanted to go, when he and Grady were hatching their original escape plan back in Grady's apartment. That now seems like a lifetime ago. He wonders if Grady is aware of the irony, as well, but doesn't ask him. If he opens his mouth to speak, he's going to choke on smoke. Instead, he focuses on leading them out of it.

The Exit isn't sure how he ended up in charge of this ragtag group. He was uncomfortable with it at first, but has now grown to accept it. After all, is it really so different than his normal work? He does what he does to protect humanity. Is that not what he's doing now? These people—his neighbors—are a part of that collective humanity. The only difference is that instead of saving them from an outside, otherworldly threat, he's saving them from their other neighbors—and perhaps from themselves. If they'll listen to him, he's certain he can see them through this night. If they don't, then they're on their own, much like Shaggy and the two men from the convenience store are right now.

He will keep them safe, he vows, as the smoke stings his eyes, making it impossible to see. He will keep them safe as long as he can, provided it doesn't lead to his own death. He will protect them, just as he protects everybody else.

And this time, it won't require a sacrifice.

The thought pleases him. It will be nice to do good without having to spill blood for a change. It will be nice not to need a sacrifice.

Finally, they pass beyond the burning ruins of their former home, and the smoke starts to dissipate. On their left now is the woods. To their right are a few more homes and garages. When the smoke has cleared enough to breathe again, the Exit halts. He lets go of Stephanie's hand and wipes his stinging eyes. When his vision returns, he surveys them.

"Is everyone okay?"

Coughing and sputtering, they nod, wiping at their eyes and noses. The Exit notices that Grady has put the gun down and is flexing his right hand, as if the appendage has gone to sleep.

"Grady?"

"I'm fine," the old man wheezes, picking up the gun. "Let's move out."

"Remember, try not to talk from here on out. We are almost to the end of the alley. When we reach Main Street, we'll be more exposed than we are here."

They all nod in understanding, even the boy, Caleb. The Exit is impressed by how well the child has endured tonight. He feels a swelling of admiration for him. He glances behind them, expecting to see Tick Tock, but there is no sign of the fat man. They haven't seen a single pursuer since they all chased after Shaggy. The Exit wonders how much longer that luck will hold out. Then he leads them forward again.

A large, yellow cat slinks out of the woods to their left, green eyes appraising them curiously. Its bushy tail hangs low to the ground, twitching slowly back and forth. The movement reminds the Exit of Tick Tock's head. The animal is obviously frightened and wary, but it doesn't flee. He admires that.

Stephanie gasps, and the Exit turns to her.

"That's one of Mrs. Carlucci's cats," she whispers. "That's Hannibal."

Before the Exit can stop her, Stephanie breaks ranks and slowly approaches the cat. The animal eyes her warily, but still doesn't retreat back into the smoke-filled woods. Stephanie crouches down and holds out one hand, wiggling her fingers. It occurs to the Exit that although the girl was worried about her nudity before, that no longer seems to be a concern. Perhaps it is the cat who has put her at ease, although he doesn't understand why. The older he gets, the more certain he becomes that he will never understand other people, and their emotions and motivations. At least, not completely.

He suddenly feels very alone.

Stephanie makes a kissing noise, wriggling her fingers more urgently. "Hannibal. Come here, kitty kitty kitty. Come on."

Hannibal takes one step forward. Then two.

"That's it." Stephanie smiles.

"Stephanie," the Exit whispers. "We don't have time for this."

"Then go on without me," she mutters, not taking her eyes off the cat.

Sighing in frustration, the Exit glances around. The alley remains deserted, but the sounds of conflict still echo across the town—faded gunshots, muted screams, car tires screeching from far away.

Hannibal seems to relax as he approaches Stephanie. He consents to let her pet his head and scratch under his chin. He walks in tiny circles, vigorously rubbing each side of his face against her outstretched fingers. His purrs grow louder with each stroke, and the Exit worries for a moment that someone might hear them. Hannibal turns again, allowing Stephanie to scratch his back. Then he walks over to the rest of the group.

As Stephanie regains her feet, Terri and Caleb pause to pet the cat. The Exit's annoyance with them grows, but he reminds himself that at least they are doing so quietly. Yes, they are creating a delay, but they aren't attracting attention— at least as far as he can determine. It was possible a lone attacker or a group of lunatics were hiding in the shadows right now, watching the entire display. But he didn't think so. From everything he'd seen so far tonight, and all of the behavior they had evidenced, the naked mob didn't seem very keen on waiting. They tended to charge ahead instead.

Except for Mrs. Carlucci's apartment, he reminds himself.

Terri motions at Grady, indicating he should pet the cat. Grady raises his hand and waves, declining the opportunity.

"I'm more of a dog person," he whispers.

The Exit clears his throat softly. They all look at him, including the cat. He cocks his head and starts walking again. The group begins to follow. Hannibal trots along at Stephanie's side, eyes darting from shadow to shadow, ears twitching. He is obviously alert, and it occurs to the Exit that maybe the cat isn't so bad to have along, after all.

They come to a two-car garage on their right that is under construction. In the yard next to it is a wooden pallet stacked high with bags of concrete, another filled with roofing tiles, and a third with loose lengths of rebar.

Well, the Exit thinks, *I saw several of them armed with rebar tonight. Now I know where they got it from.*

He grabs a length for himself. Stephanie and Terri follow suit. The Exit is pleased with these new acquisitions. The weapons will only help to serve their disguise.

The alley comes to an end at the corner of a Chinese restaurant called Fortune Garden. The Exit thinks that's a perfect omen. They could use a garden of good fortune right about now. And indeed, he spots a second good omen as they pass the rear of restaurant. Someone—he assumes probably the owner—has been growing vegetables on a small plot of dirt behind the building. Plump, ripe tomatoes dangle heavily from their vines, as do several varieties of peppers that he doesn't recognize, and something that looks like a zucchini but is bigger and rounder. The Exit glances around, listens, and then studies the cat. When Hannibal shows no signs of immediate distress, the Exit trots up a small embankment and plucks a tomato from the vine. He bites into it, relishing the taste as juice and pulp and seeds squirt into his mouth. The effect on his system is immediate. He doesn't know if it's real or merely psychological, but he feels rejuvenated and refreshed. He takes another bite. He turns silently to the others and points at the garden, asking if anyone else would like a tomato. Stephanie nods, and Terri holds up two fingers. He places his rebar to the side and picks a tomato for each of them. As he hands them down, he glances at Grady. The old man seems oblivious and disinterested.

No, the Exit decides, after a moment. *That's not what he seems. What he seems is tired.*

While the others enjoy their quick snack, he retrieves his weapon, tiptoes back down the embankment and creeps to the end of the alley. Seeing no activity in the immediate vicinity, he motions at the others to follow him. They do.

Caleb wipes tomato seeds from his chin.

The Exit turns left, stepping out onto Main Street. The others follow, their naked feet padding along softly behind him. It occurs to him then how quiet the town has now become. The sounds he'd heard a few minutes ago—the gunshots and screams and screeching tires—have all faded. Now, there is only silence. The Exit wonders if they are the only ones left alive.

They continue on, passing by a Rite-Aid and a Hardees fast food restaurant. Neither establishment has escaped unscathed. The windows are smashed and debris is scattered throughout the parking lots. Some of the debris is human. A lone naked man kneels at the restaurant's drive-thru window, calmly using a bloody hacksaw to separate the arm off a victim. He glances up at them with feral eyes. The Exit does his best to return the gesture, apparently convincing the madman. They continue on, unscathed.

A little farther up the left hand side of the street is a storm drain. The iron grating that covered it has been removed and tossed out into the road. As they walk by it, the Exit glances down. The storm drain has been filled with severed heads— men, women, children, all staring up sightlessly, mouths hanging open in death. He glances back at Terri and nods toward the hole. She manages to divert Caleb's attention from it until they are past. It occurs to the Exit that this was perhaps foolish. After all, the boy has seen a multitude of other atrocities tonight. Why should they be so concerned about him seeing this one? But if it keeps the boy quiet, and prevents him from reacting in such a way that their cover is blown, then it's better to take precautions.

Movement in the sky catches his attention. The Exit glances upward and sees the pale oval of a searchlight moving across the clouds. Then he looks at the horizon and sees that it is glowing—not from a fire or from sunrise, but from an array of bright electric lights. It's the National Guard perimeter, and he wants to cheer. Instead, he motions at it, making sure the others see. Their expressions mirror his own—relief, joy, and determination.

All except Grady's. His expression is slack. His mouth hangs open, and his eyes droop. He is limping badly, favoring his injured ankle.

The Exit touches his shoulder, staring inquisitively. Grady motions at him to keep going. Frowning, the Exit starts down the sidewalk. The others follow behind.

The houses on Main Street mirror those in the rest of the town. If anything, the damage is even more extensive here. A swath of destruction has been carved through them, and no home remains unscathed. The dead are everywhere— in the street, in cars, hanging out of windows, porches, and yards—and although the corpses are composed of both sides in tonight's war, those wearing clothes far outnumber the naked.

They pass an empty State Police car, tipped over on its driver's side. The vehicle leaks gasoline and oil and antifreeze onto the road. They find a second police car half a block away from the first. This one remains upright, but it has been flattened by what the Exit can only assume were a pack of crazies armed with sledgehammers. The roof is even with the hood of the car, and the doors and side panels have collapsed. The two state troopers inside the vehicle are even flatter than the car itself—recognizable only by their blood-soaked uniforms.

Gunfire echoes ahead of them, from somewhere in the direction of the perimeter, shattering the stillness. Judging by the sound, it's a heavy caliber automatic weapon. A National Guardsman holding the line, perhaps? The sound gives him hope. Safety is at hand. And if not safety, then at least shelter. At least a brief respite.

All they have to do is make it there.

That's when Grady collapses, crumpling to the pavement like a falling leaf. The Exit cringes at the sound the old man's head makes as it strikes the pavement. The pistol clatters out into the street and slides under the rear tire of a parked car. The bullets he'd carried in his other hand are scattered across the road and sidewalk. The others cry out in surprise and dismay. Casting aside their rebar clubs, they rush to him, all pretense of disguising themselves gone.

The Exit pushes his way through the others and crouches down next to Grady. He is surprised to discover that he feels concern for his neighbor, and is even more surprised by the relief that washes over him when he sees that Grady's eyes are open and alert. The old man's expression is one of agony, and he claws weakly at his chest.

"My...heart..."

"I'll carry you." The Exit slides one arm under the elderly man's legs.

"Bullshit," Grady rasps. "Can't go...anymore, Mendez. I'm done."

"No, you're not. We are less than a mile from the perimeter. I can carry you that far."

Grimacing, Grady waves his hand. "Slow you...down."

"His head," Stephanie whispers.

The Exit sees blood spreading out onto the sidewalk from beneath Grady's head. He scowls, feeling a rage build inside of him.

"I don't..." the Exit pauses. "I don't have anybody, Grady. In my life, I mean. There's no one. I'm alone. And yet...there is you. I have you."

Stephanie, Terri, and Caleb stare at him. Grady looks up, smiling.

"Listen to me...Mendez. Everything I had...burned up tonight...in that...fire. I've got nothing...except my daughter. She's out there…somewhere. You all need to make it…out of here and… tell her. All I have is her and…the rest of you. I need you to go on…"

"You are coming with us," the Exit insists. Then he turns to the others. "Help me lift him. We have to do it carefully."

"No…"

Grady's pained expression is replaced with one of resolve. He raises one trembling, liver-spotted hand and points back toward town. The others turn to look.

Tick Tock is a block away, limping toward them, at the head of a pack two-dozen strong, if not more.

Hissing, Hannibal turns and runs into the night, leaving the others behind. The Exit stares after the cat for a second, and then turns his attention back to Grady.

"Never did…trust cats…" Grady groans.

"Hurry," the Exit says, and slips his other hand beneath Grady's shoulders. He feels warm, sticky blood on his fingers.

"Goddamn it," Grady wheezes. "Leave me…be and get… going."

"What happened to no man left behind, Grady?"

"What happened to…you can't die…Mendez?"

The Exit pauses. He looks into the old man's eyes. Grady smiles, nods slightly, and then grimaces in pain.

"You can't…die tonight. Now…prop me up against… that car… and…find my gun…"

Nodding, the Exit does as he asks. Grady moans, biting his lip as the Exit lifts him from the ground and carries him over to the car. Caleb ducks down and retrieves the gun, holding it with an expression of awe. Terri snatches it away from him and hands it to the Exit.

"Get going," he tells them. "I'll be right behind you."

Nodding, Terri grabs Caleb's hand and leads him toward the searchlights.

"You, too," the Exit tells Stephanie.

She hesitates, then leans down and kisses Grady on the top of his head. "Thank you."

He smiles. "That's a…nice way for an…old guy like me…to go out. Kiss from a…pretty lady."

Stephanie's face twists with grief. She rushes away, sobbing. She bends down and grabs her weapon. Her shoulders hitch as she then runs after Terri and Caleb.

Tick Tock roars. The Exit glances behind them and sees the mob surge forward.

"Go…" Grady urges.

The Exit hands him the gun. Then he turns, searching for the scattered bullets.

"There's no time," Grady insists. "I'm loaded. It will be enough."

"I was wrong," the Exit tells him.

Grady looks up at him quizzically.

"I was wrong," the Exit repeats. "I thought it would be different tonight. I thought that I wouldn't need a sacrifice to save everyone this time."

Grady stares at him for a moment. Then he coughs.

"Anybody ever…tell you…you're a weird little fucker… Mendez?"

Smiling, the Exit reaches down and pats his head. "Thank you, Grady."

Nodding, Grady raises the gun with one trembling hand and points it at the onrushing horde.

The Exit runs after the others. He flinches when he hears the first gunshot behind him, but he doesn't turn around to look.

It isn't until his vision grows blurry that he realizes he is crying.

Twenty-Four

Stephanie, The Exit, Terri, and Caleb: City Limits

Stephanie hears four shots as she runs, echoing over the enraged cries of their pursuers. She doesn't turn around, but she flinches when she hears Grady cry out in pain. Then, his cries are lost, buried beneath the others—but those are not cries of pain. They are cries of savage joy and exultation. And of rage.

She leaps over a body sprawled in the road—a dead nun, still dressed in her full habit. Two dinner forks stick out of her eyes. Laughter wells up inside her but she forces it down. She remembers a joke from grade school—what's black and white and red and runs into walls? A nun with forks in her eyes.

She glances at a light post to her right and sees a man dangling from a noose made from an extension cord. His legs kick feebly, but she convinces herself that it's just the wind making them move.

The bank and the used car lot to her left are both on fire. Stephanie takes a deep breath and holds it as she barrels through a cloud of smoke drifting across the street. Her eyes sting, but she pushes on until the smoke passes. When she exhales, her chest aches.

Grady's last words run through her mind. He called her a pretty lady. That was what he saw her as. That was his perception. She sobs, feeling gratitude and fear and happiness and regret all at the same time.

She runs past destroyed houses and wrecked cars and dead bodies, fleeing toward the lights growing ever brighter and bigger ahead of them, and thinks about Grady's words again. They give her strength, and strength is what she needs, because her lungs are burning and her legs feel like she's running through cement. Her head pounds in time with her pulse.

He called me a pretty lady...

She wonders how the others perceive her. She thinks about how she perceived them, before tonight. Mrs. Carlucci, for example. She'd always been the old lady next door, the one who acted nice, but also a little nervous. Before tonight, Stephanie had always assumed that nervousness was a silent form of disapproval over her transition, but she's not so sure about that anymore. And never in a million years would she have thought the old lady would be so resourceful in the face of danger. The way she'd helped, fearlessly going up against their attackers...

Stephanie realizes that her initial perceptions of Mrs. Carlucci were all wrong. She was wrong about a lot of them. Sam, for instance. And Turo. Yes, Shaggy had behaved exactly as she'd expected him to, even calling her a he-she at one point, but Turo had been surprisingly kind and accepting—in his way. And Sam... Sam had called her Steph. She still thinks she'd prefer to be Rose, but Steph felt good. It felt...acceptable.

All of them are gone now. Gone just as she'd gotten to know them.

She hates that this night—this hell—was the catalyst for her to finally break those misconceptions, and truly get to know the people around her.

She hears someone stumble behind her, followed by a gasp from Terri. Stephanie turns around and sees Caleb sprawled on the sidewalk, hands splayed. He's picking himself up, bottom lip puckering as he notices a bleeding scrape on his knee. Then Mendez appears beside the boy and, without pausing, scoops him up and continues running, passing by both Stephanie and Terri.

"Hurry," he pants. "They're gaining on us!"

Stephanie sees that he is right. Grady may have taken a few of their pursuers with him, but their numbers haven't thinned. The naked horde charges after them, filling the street. Tick Tock lopes along behind the procession, arms outstretched as if to welcome them in his embrace.

Stephanie turns and runs. She grits her teeth and focuses only on breathing. She passes Terri, draws alongside Mendez, and then she's in the lead again, racing toward the perimeter.

The spotlights fill the road ahead of them now. A wall of sandbags has been erected. Behind the wall is a line of military vehicles, fire trucks, and police cars parked nose to nose and blocking the road. Uniformed guardsmen and various members of the local and state police stand in a phalanx between the sandbags and the vehicles. She notices that there are some civilians among them, as well, helping to man the post. All of them—civilian, law enforcement, and military—are armed. Their weapons are raised, and they're shouting something, but Stephanie's pulse is so loud in her ears that she can't understand them.

She screams, urging herself forward as a sudden pain jolts through the calf of her right leg. It burns, coursing through her entire body. Behind her, the cries of the horde grow louder. Ahead, the soldier's shouts do the same.

It occurs to her then how they must look. She, Terri, Caleb, and Mendez are naked and dirty, running ahead of a naked and dirty mob. She tosses the rebar aside, presenting herself as weaponless, and hoping that they will notice.

See us for who we are, she thinks as they near the blockade. *See us for who we really are…*

One of the guardsmen shouts into a bullhorn. They're close enough now that she can see their expressions. Everything behind them is lost in the glare of the spotlights, but she can see their faces clearly, and their weapons.

Weapons that are pointed at her and her neighbors.

Faces and expressions that mirror the fear and desperation she feels.

"We're not them," she shrieks. "Don't shoot. We're not like them!"

The horde are right behind them now. Stephanie can hear their grunts of exertion, the sound of their teeth snapping, their weapons clanging.

See us for who we are...

See us for who we are...

See us for who we are...

She's still thinking it when the first gunshot rings out.

Afterword

I got the idea for this short novel when a naked man rode a bicycle past my home one morning in 2013.

I used to live in a remote cabin nestled on a mountaintop in the Susquehanna River bottoms. There were a few other homes in the valley below me, as well as a winding, twisting, one-lane road that seemed to flood out every time it rained—after which the valley would fill with fog. It was an eerie, spooky place, as rural as you can get for Pennsylvania, and perfectly suited to both my writing and my lifestyle. My friends affectionately referred to the area as Shoggoth Town. If you're a regular listener to my podcast, then you've no doubt heard them talk about it on many occasions. And yes, I'll admit, Shoggoth Town was an apt name, but I didn't mind. I liked living there. I liked having privacy and space and a backyard full of black bears and deer. The few neighbors were all fairly normal, and I knew them all quite well.

I was awake at five in the morning the day I saw the naked man. This wasn't abnormal. Since I'm at my most productive early in the day, I always get up at five. I was still in bed, talking to my girlfriend on the phone and getting ready to exercise and then start writing, when I happened to glance out the window. There, down below, on that twisted, narrow little road, was a naked man on an old ten-speed bicycle. I paused, making sure my eyes weren't playing tricks on me, and verifying that I was indeed awake. I asked my girlfriend to verify this, too, which she did. Then I told her what I was seeing. She took it in stride.

Deciding to investigate, I told her that I'd call her back.

I hopped out of bed, clad only in a pair of boxer shorts, grabbed a pistol from my gun safe (deciding it would be prudent to approach this naked stranger with some precaution) and headed out the door. My driveway was a slim, rutted gravel road that wound down the mountain. As I walked down it, I kept catching glimpses of the nude bicyclist through the trees. Unfortunately, by the time I got to the bottom, he was gone.

At the time, it seemed like every week the mainstream media were reporting on another case where some drug-crazed nut tore off his or her clothes and ran rampant through the streets. In most of these cases, the perpetrator attempted to break into homes or vehicles or places of business. In several cases, they attacked other people. Several victims died.

Walking back up the mountain, still wearing my boxer shorts, I started thinking about what would happen if there was suddenly a horde of such fiends. Then that idea went to live in the back of my brain, which is where all of my ideas go. The good ones eventually get written down. The bad ones dissipate like dreams.

Life went on.

In early 2014, my cabin and many of the other homes in the valley were destroyed during a series of severe winter storms. Meteorologists called it the Polar Vortex. We called it Hell. We'd survived multiple floods and blizzards over the years, but the Polar Vortex did us in. My place was pretty much uninhabitable afterward, and after seeing the impact the situation had on my youngest son, I decided that maybe a remote mountaintop cabin overlooking Shoggoth Town wasn't the best place to raise a seven-year old. So, he and I packed up our belongings (except for the stuff destroyed in the storms) and moved into an apartment complex in a nearby town. My son was much happier with this living arrangement, and I was happy that he was happy.

We'd been in the complex for about a month, and I was smoking a cigar one day, and thinking about how I viewed my new neighbors (none of whom I really knew) and how they viewed me (a new tenant whom they didn't know) versus how I viewed myself and how they probably viewed themselves.

Then I remembered the naked man on the bicycle.

And that's how this novel came to be—a story about our self-perceptions versus other people's perceptions of us. And about how we don't really know our neighbors anymore. And about deranged naked people on a killing spree.

Javier Mendez, aka The Exit, has appeared in several of my short stories—"I Am An Exit", "This Is Not An Exit" and "Exit Strategies". He also appears in my novel, *The Seven.* An alternate reality version of Grady Hicks has previously appeared in a short story called "Customer Service Letter Written by an Angry Old Man on Christmas Eve". Hannibal the cat previously appeared in a short story called "Halves". A few paragraphs of the introductory chapter with Sam were cannibalized from a short story I wrote called "The Eleventh Muse".

Some of you will no doubt notice that I departed from my usual style of narrative voice, and chose something different for this novel. I'm not sure why that happened. It just did. That's how the story wanted to be told, so that's how I told it.

Writers are weird as fuck.

It's also worth noting that, just like in many of my other novels, while most of the towns and locations in this book are real, I have taken certain geographical liberties with them. So don't go looking for the Pine Village Apartment Complex in Red Lion, PA. You won't find it. And if you did, you wouldn't like what comes creeping across the parking lot after dark.

As always, thank you for your support. If you keep reading them, I'll keep writing them.

Brian Keene
August 2015

BRIAN KEENE writes novels, comic books, short fiction, and occasional journalism for money. He is the author of over forty books, mostly in the horror, crime, and dark fantasy genres. His 2003 novel, *The Rising*, is often credited (along with Robert Kirkman's *The Walking Dead* comic and Danny Boyle's *28 Days Later* film) with inspiring pop culture's current interest in zombies. In addition to his own original work, Keene has written for media properties such as *Doctor Who, The X-Files, Hellboy, Masters of the Universe*, and *Superman*.

Several of Keene's novels have been developed for film, including *Ghoul, The Ties That Bind*, and *Fast Zombies Suck*. Several more are in-development or under option. Keene also oversees Maelstrom, his own small press publishing imprint specializing in collectible limited editions, via Thunderstorm Books.

Keene's work has been praised in such diverse places as *The New York Times, The History Channel, The Howard Stern Show, CNN.com, Publisher's Weekly, Media Bistro, Fangoria Magazine*, and *Rue Morgue Magazine*. He has won numerous awards and honors, including the World Horror Grand Master award, two Bram Stoker awards, and a recognition from Whiteman A.F.B. (home of the B-2 Stealth Bomber) for his outreach to U.S. troops serving both overseas and abroad. A prolific public speaker, Keene has delivered talks at conventions, college campuses, theaters, and inside Central Intelligence Agency headquarters in Langley, VA.

The father of two sons, Keene lives in rural Pennsylvania.

deadite press

"Earthworm Gods" Brian Keene - One day, it starts raining-and never stops. Global super-storms decimate the planet, eradicating most of mankind. Pockets of survivors gather on mountaintops, watching as the waters climb higher and higher. But as the tides rise, something else is rising, too. Now, in the midst of an ecological nightmare, the remnants of humanity face a new menace, in a battle that stretches from the rooftops of submerged cities to the mountaintop islands jutting from the sea. The old gods are dead. Now is the time of the Earthworm Gods...

"Earworm Gods: Selected Scenes from the End of the World" Brian Keene - a collection of short stories set in the world of Earthworm Gods and Earthworm Gods II: Deluge. From the first drop of rain to humanity's last waterlogged stand, these tales chronicle the fall of man against a horrifying, unstoppable evil. And as the waters rise over the United States, the United Kingdom, Australia, New Zealand, and elsewhere-brand new monsters surface-along with some familiar old favorites, to wreak havoc on an already devastated mankind..

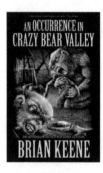

"An Occurrence in Crazy Bear Valley" Brian Keene- The Old West has never been weirder or wilder than it has in the hands of master horror writer Brian Keene. Morgan and his gang are on the run--from their pasts and from the posse riding hot on their heels, intent on seeing them hang. But when they take refuge in Crazy Bear Valley, their flight becomes a siege as they find themselves battling a legendary race of monstrous, bloodthirsty beings. Now, Morgan and his gang aren't worried about hanging. They just want to live to see the dawn.

"Entombed II" Brian Keene- It has been several months since the disease known as Hamelin's Revenge decimated the world. Civilization has collapsed and the dead far outnumber the living. The survivors seek refuge from the roaming zombie hordes, but one-by-one, those shelters are falling.Twenty-five survivors barricade themselves inside a former military bunker buried deep beneath a luxury hotel. They are safe from the zombies...but are they safe from one another?

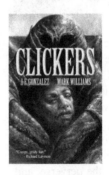

deadite press

"WZMB" Andre Duza - It's the end of the world, but we're not going off the air! Martin Stone was a popular shock jock radio host before the zombie apocalypse. Then for six months the dead destroyed society. Humanity is now slowly rebuilding and Martin Stone is back to doing what he does best-taking to the airwaves. Host of the only radio show in this new world, he helps organize other survivors. But zombies aren't the only threat. There are others that thought humanity needed to end.

"Tribesmen" Adam Cesare - Thirty years ago, cynical sleazeball director Tito Bronze took a tiny cast and crew to a desolate island. His goal: to exploit the local tribes, spray some guts around, cash in on the gore-spattered 80s Italian cannibal craze. But the pissed-off spirits of the island had other ideas. And before long, guts were squirting behind the scenes, as well. While the camera kept rolling...

"Wet and Screaming" Shane McKenzie - From a serial killer's yard sale to a hoarder's hideous secret. From a cartoon character made real to a man addicted to car accidents. From a bloody Halloween to child murder as a means for saving the world. The rules of normalcy and society no longer apply - you're now in a place of cruelty, terror, and things that go bump in the night. In Shane McKenzie's first collection - he explores the horrific, the grotesque, the perverse, and the downright bizarre in ten short stories.

"Suffer the Flesh" Monica J. O'Rourke - Zoey always wished she was thinner. One day she meets a strange woman who informs her of an ultimate weight-loss program, and Zoey is quickly abducted off the streets of Manhattan and forced into this program. Zoey's enrolling whether she wants to or not. Held hostage with many other women, Zoey is forced into degrading acts of perversion for the amusement of her captors. ...

"The Haunter of the Threshold" Edward Lee - There is something very wrong with this backwater town. Suicide notes, magic gems, and haunted cabins await her. Plus the woods are filled with monsters, both human and otherworldly. And then there are the horrible tentacles . . . Soon Hazel is thrown into a battle for her life that will test her sanity and sex drive. The sequel to H.P. Lovecraft's The Haunter of the Dark is Edward Lee's most pornographic novel to date!

"Boot Boys of the Wolf Reich" David Agranoff - PIt is the summer of 1989 and they spend their days hanging out and having fun, and their nights fighting the local neo-Nazi gangs. Driven back and badly beaten, the local Nazi contingent finds the strangest of allies - The last survivor of a cult of Nazi werewolf assassins. An army of neo-Nazi werewolves are just what he needs. But first, they have some payback for all those meddling Anti-racist SHARPs...

"The Dark Ones" Bryan Smith - They are The Dark Ones. The name began as a self-deprecating joke, but it stuck and now it's a source of pride. They're the one who don't fit in. The misfits who drink and smoke too much and stay out all hours of the night. Everyone knows they're trouble. On the outskirts of Ransom, TN is an abandoned, boarded-up house. Something evil happened there long ago. The evil has been contained there ever since, locked down tight in the basement—until the night The Dark Ones set it free . . .

"Genital Grinder" Ryan Harding - *"Think you're hardcore? Think again. If you've handled everything Edward Lee, Wrath James White, and Bryan Smith have thrown at you, then put on your rubber parka, spread some plastic across the floor, and get ready for Ryan Harding, the unsung master of hardcore horror. Abandon all hope, ye who enter here. Harding's work is like an acid bath, and pain has never been so sweet."*
- Brian Keene

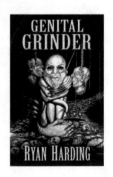

AVAILABLE FROM AMAZON.COM